DR. SEUSS

Illustrated by Meryl Henderson

DR. SEUSS
Young Author and Artist

by Kathleen Kudlinski

ALADDIN PAPERBACKS

New York   London   Toronto   Sydney

**To Paul and Ruby Pinders at Crown Point Camping
Area, VT, where this book was written (at RV site 29),
and to Adam and Ryan Beal. —K. V. K.**

❧

ALADDIN PAPERBACKS
An imprint of Simon & Schuster Children's Publishing Division
1230 Avenue of the Americas, New York, NY 10020
Text copyright © 2005 by Kathleen Kudlinski
Illustrations copyright © 2005 by Meryl Henderson
All rights reserved, including the right of
reproduction in whole or in part in any form.
ALADDIN PAPERBACKS, CHILDHOOD OF FAMOUS AMERICANS,
and colophon are registered trademarks of Simon & Schuster, Inc.
Designed by Lisa Vega
The text of this book was set in New Caledonia.
Manufactured in the United States of America
First Aladdin Paperbacks edition June 2005
2 4 6 8 10 9 7 5 3 1
Library of Congress Control Number 2004113720
ISBN 0-689-87347-6

ILLUSTRATIONS

CONTENTS

Happy Birthday!

Ted crouched behind the parlor door, trying not to giggle out loud. He rested a warning hand on his pit bull's head. Rex quivered with excitement. Marnie sat practicing scales on the piano, pretending not to know about her brother's mischief.

The sound of their mother's footsteps floated down the hall. Ted held his breath until she passed the door.

"Boo!" He jumped out, waving his arms. Rex leaped alongside, barking.

"*Ach, mein* heart!" Mrs. Geisel grabbed

her chest. The fairy wings on her shoulders bobbed wildly. She staggered through the parlor past the big new radio, around the piano bench, and past the fireplace. "Quick! My fairy dust!" she gasped. Then she twirled about and fell onto the couch. Rex jumped up to comfort her, a blur of black and white patches and red, licking tongue.

"Stop fooling, *Mutter*!" Marnie laughed. "Teddy's guests will be here soon!" She turned a page in her practice book and started to play the piano again.

Mrs. Geisel stood quickly and straightened her fairy costume. "Marnie, you know the rules. German only spoken here," she said firmly. "Use your English elsewhere." She tapped Ted on the head with her magic wand as she hurried into the kitchen.

"*Ach, nein!*" she screamed from the other room. "Theodor Seuss Geisel, you scallywag!"

"What did you do now?" Marnie asked.

Ted just grinned. "You'll see in a minute,"

he said. Mrs. Geisel stormed out of the kitchen. In her hand was a brown toy dog. On its head was Mrs. Geisel's new church hat. "But *Mutter*," he explained in German, "Theophrastus asked nicely if he could come to my tenth birthday party. I told him he'd have to wear a costume, like everybody else."

Mrs. Geisel jerked her long hatpins out of her hat and smoothed its quivering feathers. "This is not a costume," she scolded.

"It is if you are a dog. Theophrastus told me he wanted to come dressed as the very best mother in the whole wide world." Ted snuck a wink at his sister.

Marnie groaned loudly. Rex cocked his head. Mrs. Geisel stood frozen. A mix of anger and humor and pride flickered across her face. Finally she laughed. "Ted, you may be dressed in long pants for the day, but there is nothing adult about this prank."

"He'll be back in his little-boy knickers tomorrow," Marnie said, looking prim. She

added, "I don't think his humor will ever grow up."

"In a way I hope it doesn't," Mrs. Geisel said as she headed back into the kitchen. "Ted, it is time to go and meet your *Vater*. Then the party can begin."

Ted snapped his fingers and Rex bounded to join him. Through the top half of the carved wooden front door, Ted tried to listen for the trolley car's bell. Hearing anything over the noisy streets was hopeless. The whole street seemed to be a party. Horses' hooves clopped, wagon wheels screeched, Model Ts chugged and honked, church bells pealed, street vendors yelled, and peacocks screamed from the zoo down the block. Over all of that, the mills made a steady clanking and roaring. Ted grinned. He loved the energy of Springfield, Massachusetts.

Everything happened here. Two hundred trains arrived at the station daily. Smith & Wesson made enough new guns to fill a

United States Armory. The second commercial radio station in the country had just begun broadcasting from the hotel downtown. They were building the biggest bridge ever across the Connecticut River.

It was March 2, 1914, and he was finally ten. He pulled himself up, opened the bottom half of the door, and strode onto the porch dressed at last as a man. He snapped his fingers and Rex bounded out, too. The pit bull's wagging tail whipping against his leg hit fabric instead of woolen stockings. It felt strange. *Vater's* bowler hat pressed against his head in a way that everyday caps never did. Ted took a puff on an imaginary cigar, then pretended to pop open a fine pocket watch. "*Vater*," he practiced. "You are late."

This evening he did not slide down the railing, choosing the stairs instead. He strolled down the street touching his hat brim to the women he passed. Mrs. Kaufman struggled with a smile. "Good day, Mrs. Kaufman," Ted said. Mrs. Hessledorf simply stared. "*Guten Tag, Frau* Hesseldorf," Ted said, and moved on.

But Mrs. Haynes scolded him. "For shame, Theodor. Does your father know you are playing in his clothes?"

"No ma'am," Ted mumbled.

As she passed, Ted heard her threaten, "Wait until the ladies in the club hear of this."

Ted kept on walking. Old Lady Haynes and her friends would not drink his father's beer, so they didn't matter. He reached the street corner and squinted down the block toward Mulberry Street. The trolley was late.

Ted stood still and pretended to be a starving orphan. He felt his shoulders sag in sorrow and his stomach rumble in hunger. When Rex sat down beside him and licked his hand, Ted jumped. In his imagination, the friendly pit bull became a wolf. This wolf would adopt him into the pack and poor, orphaned Ted would become king of the wolves. He was trying to imagine where the wolf's den might be hidden in Forest Park when the trolley bell rang. Ted shook his head and focused on meeting his father.

Normally he ran to hug *Vater* and beg for the funny papers. Today, Ted wore grown-up clothes. He decided to act differently. He stood quietly, watching his father lightly take the big step to the curb. Other commuters waddled or shuffled homeward, tired and rumpled from a day's work. Not *Vater*! Mr. Geisel's suit was still clean, his shirt starched and tidy. It made Ted stand taller, just to look at his energetic father. *Vater* was a tall man with a flat belly, wide shoulders, dark hair, and a huge, walrussy moustache.

"Well, a good day to you, sir," Mr. Geisel said to his son. The moustache hid any smile, but his eyes crinkled up with glee. He shook Theodor's hand firmly. "You are looking quite dapper today."

"*Willkommen, Vater,*" Ted said. "How was your day at the brewery?"

"Never mind that, my boy! You are ten, ten at last, fully ten!" Ted stood even straighter, tall and slender like his father. "Teddy, you will never guess what I have for you this year, son. A true birthday surprise!"

Ted did not have to guess. "A gun, *Vater*?"

"Ho, ho, ho—yes!"

Ted felt himself squeezed in a great cigar-scented hug. "We'll make a marksman of you yet!" Mr. Geisel looked across the street. "There is Cousin Bette and her little ones. We'd better hurry home. Wouldn't do to have the host arrive after his guests!"

The Geisels raced each other up the street, Rex barking at their heels. The music room was already a sea of young cousins in white party clothes. The girls wore starched white bows on their heads and white skirts, socks, and petticoats. The boys were in fresh white knickers and suspenders. The littlest boys even wore white caps. Marnie was playing piano for the crowd, though no one was listening.

They were all chattering in German. There were over a thousand families in Springfield with family roots in Germany. That meant five thousand children. Some had just arrived in the United States. Most, like Ted's grandparents, the Seusses and Geisels, had great-grandparents from the old country. Other families had lived in Massachusetts for many more generations. All of the city's schools taught German. The Springfield library had a whole section of books in German. One church held services in German, and most stores carried German foods and newspapers. And most homes like Ted's were full of the hearty, guttural sound of the German language.

Ted escaped to the front parlor. It was choked with cigar smoke and uncles, men from the health club his *Grossvater* Seuss had helped found, and *Grossvater* Geisel.

Ted smiled. This was where he belonged now—with the men. When he finally noticed Ted, *Grossvater* Geisel spread his arms wide. "The birthday boy," he roared. Ted found himself suffocated against his grandfather's enormous belly. His face was ground against a watch chain. Ted tried to wiggle free.

Grossvater's arms squeezed tighter. Deep in the chest beside his ear, Ted heard the rumble of laughter begin. "This little whippersnapper thinks he's a man today!" The whole belly shook with great guffaws. Ted fought for breath and began snapping his fingers for Rex.

"Rouf!" At the dog's threatening bark, *Grossvater*'s arms loosened.

"Well, well," *Grossvater* said. "It's a wise man who makes good friends and keeps them close."

"Then I am a wise man?" Ted asked. He straightened his father's jacket and flushed at the sound of chuckles around the room.

"I certainly hope so, Little Ted. Someday you'll have the whole brewery," *Grossvater* said. "But Big Ted gets it first." Now the room filled with congratulations and the sound of backslapping. *Grossvater* held up his hands. "Not so fast!" he said. "I'm in no hurry to give the business to my son. Four, five years and we'll talk."

Ted stood still. He had never seriously thought about what he would do with his life. Suddenly, there it was, all planned out. *Grossvater* would give the brewery to *Vater*. And *Vater* would pass it on to him. The factory. The beer wagons and horses. The customers. A trolley ride to work every day. Ted wasn't sure he wanted all of this. The men crowded close to *Grossvater* and began discussing their business plans. *His* business plans. Ted suddenly needed air. He wormed his way out of the huddle and fled to the hall.

The hall was full of cousins, marching single file. The strange parade was heading up the stairs. Ted whooped with delight and raced to the head of the line.

On beyond the second floor the children climbed, into the great drafty attic. The wardrobe trunks were already thrown open. Mrs. Geisel settled quarrels as children chose their costumes. Her wings were drooping, but at nearly six feet tall, she towered over everyone. No one dared to question her. Sisters and brothers helped transform each other with rabbit ears, tiger skins, frontier shirts, and cowgirl skirts. The party that came back down to the dining room table was a wild group of animals, princesses, policemen, and one ten-year-old, future brewery president.

Ted sat at the head of the great oak table. The housekeeper, Anne, had made all his favorite foods. Besides sauerkraut, the tangy, salted cabbage dish, there were five kinds of meat: bratwurst, knockwurst, liverwurst, Wiener schnitzel, and frankfurters. Sweet

applesauce and mountains of boiled potatoes filled out the menu. The dark breads at dinner and the birthday cake came from the Seuss Bakery. *"Danke,"* Ted said, thanking *Grossvater* Seuss across the table.

After dinner, they played pin-the-tail-on-the-donkey and charades. They all sang around the piano as Mrs. Geisel played. Ted played piano, too, and a little mandolin. Then it was gift time. *"Danke,"* Ted said again and again. The gun his father gave him was good enough to use in competition. *Vater* also gave him a new fishing rod. *Mutter* gave him colored pencils and pads of drawing paper.

"No more drawing on the wall," she said, smiling. Ted blushed. It had been years since he had lain in bed drawing animals on his wall when he couldn't sleep. But Mrs. Geisel had other gifts for him, too.

"That's a baby book!" Marnie sniffed as Ted pulled the paper off a new copy of *The Bad Child's Book of Beasts*. "Though it might finally teach him some manners." Ted was already thumbing through the familiar pages.

"It's not for the rhymes, you know," *Mutter* said. Ted smiled back at his mother. He had always loved the wild beasts Ian Blackwood drew to illustrate Hilaire Belloc's playful rhymes. Now he could study his own copy. *Mutter* also gave him the newest book in *The Rover Boys* series.

"You lucky stiff!" one cousin said. "Can I borrow that as soon as you're done?"

Ted agreed, and then started in on the rest of the mountain of presents.

"A slingshot!" Ted gaped at his sister. "Thanks, Marnie. You have forgiven me, then?"

They both knew what he was talking about. At her birthday, he had hidden an old brick inside a dozen different layers of fancy wrappings. It had taken Marnie half an hour to untie all the bows and find the joke inside. There was a real gift, of course—a silver pen.

But that came afterward. "That was a pretty good one, Ted," she admitted.

He went back to opening gifts. His cousins' packages held toys of every kind and sweets. A battered package from his distant German cousins held little tin soldiers for his collection. The adults sang and talked for a while. The littlest ones began to whine and yawn.

Finally, it was over. The costumes lay in a great pile for Anne to carry back upstairs. Ted spent time admiring the new gun with his father. He even walked upstairs to look at his father's shooting trophies again. But it was hard to concentrate. A picture filled his head. Ted couldn't wait to use his new pencils to draw Theophrastus wearing his mother's fancy new church hat.

Our Zoo

A year later, Mr. Geisel urged Ted to be athletic. "Ted, as I always say, physical discipline builds character. A weak body means a weak mind. German Americans show their pride in everything they do."

"Yes, *Vater*," Ted always responded dutifully. He looked out at the summer morning. The sky was full of smoke. Coal smoke, wood smoke, smoke from the dumps and power plants. But there was a fair breeze and blue sky peeked beyond. Ted knew his friends were waiting for him down the street. He tried not to squirm. *Vater's* lectures were usually short, and his father had to go to the brewery soon.

Marnie and Mrs. Geisel quietly stole away from the breakfast table. Ted watched them leave, wishing he could escape, too.

"You did your sit-ups this morning?" Mr. Geisel prompted. Ted nodded. "Push-ups? Deep knee bends and stretches?" Ted flexed a muscle for his father. "Good." *Vater* nodded. "I thought we might spend time together this weekend." Ted felt his shoulders slump. That meant endless sports drills and shooting with the men. However, *Vater* had a surprise. "Would you like to ride on the beer wagon with me today?"

Ted jumped up out of his seat. "Yes! Oh, yes, *Vater!*"

"Wash your hands and face and behind your ears, too. Check your shirt collar. You'll be on display for the brewery, you know."

❖   ❖   ❖   ❖

By the time they got to the stables, the massive Clydesdale horses were all in harnesses. Ted reached up to pat the lead mare's soft, whiskery muzzle. Her hot breath smelled like sweet grass and grain. Ted looked down. The long silky feathers around her hooves dragged on the ground. When he ran his fingers through the pale hairs, she lifted a hoof larger than his head and shook it. "A big brute like you—you're ticklish?" Ted asked, laughing. He backed up quickly.

He knew to stay out of the way as the grooms scurried about, tightening buckles and checking the heavy yokes on each animal's neck. The horse's tails were knotted up, and one groom quickly retied the ribbons in the lead mare's mane.

At last, the eight horses were ready and the wagon was attached. The other horses whinnied restlessly from their stalls. Workers hauled huge wooden kegs of beer from the warehouse. They hoisted them onto the flat wagon bed. A driver arrived, dressed in brewery colors. Gold letters across his back and painted on the side of the wagon read LIBERTY BREWERING COMPANY, SPRINGFIELD, MASSACHUSETTS. The driver hopped up onto the front seat and took the reins. "When you are ready, *Herr* Geisel," he said.

Ted clambered up behind his father. He had barely sat down on the second bench when the enormous stable doors swung open. The driver slapped the reins, and the wagon jerked ahead.

Ted loved delivering beer. People on the streets stopped to watch the horses. Children waved back when he saluted them. Traffic had to move aside to let them pass. The noise of the enormous horseshoes clanking on cobblestones echoed off the buildings on both sides of the streets. The harness bells jingled, too. It was almost like being in a parade.

When they pulled up to the bar of a hotel, it became real work. "Move, Teddy," Mr. Geisel said, urging him to help as *Vater* and the driver toppled barrels to their sides. Then they rolled them to the end of the wagon. Bartenders grabbed the kegs and rolled them into the building. Then they hurried back out to talk with the next president of the Liberty Brewery.

"We need more light ales and dark. Might even think about three deliveries a week," Mr. Smith said. "Guests at the hotel can't get enough of your Liberty brews!" Ted listened as long as he could, and then imagined the rest of the parade.

It was not hard to picture. The beer wagon took part in Springfield's many celebrations. The fire wagons, ambulances for people or for horses, and zoo cages were all pulled through the streets by horse teams. Bands and drumming corps marched in between. The newest automobiles carried the mayor and his men. Clubs marched, too. Church groups and Masons, Boy Scouts, and even a few of the new Girl Scouts joined the parades.

So did the Suffragettes, people who thought that women should have the right to vote just like men did. Many in the crowd laughed at them. There were even more jokes about the Temperance Society Ladies. Mrs. Haynes and her friends were in this group. These women wanted to make everyone stop drinking beer and alcohol! The "devil's brew," they called it.

Ted liked parade animals better. He imagined lions and tigers in cages in the parade following his beer wagon. He had to grin, picturing lions and tigers *pulling* cages instead of being locked inside them. The cages might hold . . . he thought a moment, and then finished his mental picture. Poodles! Fussy little poodlelike dogs with pink hair. Lime-green ostriches, too. Turtles could be the drivers, and . . .

The feel of his father settling into the seat brought him back to real life. "Thank you for your business!" Mr. Geisel called. At the next stop, it was, "See you after the weekend!" and the beer wagon jerked ahead again. Sometimes they met milk wagons or meat wagons. An ice wagon lumbered up one hill in front of them, lugging chunks of ice cut from the ponds in winter. Each merchant seemed to know Mr. Geisel, and they all paused to talk. Instead of being home at midday, Ted and Mr. Geisel barely arrived in time for supper.

"Where have you two been?" *Mutter* pulled Ted aside. "Did you get along with your *Vater* all day?"

"Yes, *Mutter*," Ted said. "I will draw you our parade after we eat."

"*Wunderbar!*" *Mutter* clapped her hands together.

During supper, Mr. Geisel told Ted he would like to spend Saturday with him, too. "Just us men."

"At the club?" Ted winced.

"Not all day. I have to putter in the workshop first," *Vater* said. "We will have fun."

Ted was not sure what "fun" meant to his father besides working and competing at sports. His mother caught his eye and began nodding at him. There did not seem to be a choice. "Yes, sir," he said, and the deal was made.

Mr. Geisel laid out Saturday's plans as he opened the door to the workshop. "As soon as we're through in the shop, Teddy, we'll go to the Turnverein Sports Club. We'll have a good workout there. Then we will spend a few hours at the Schützenverein riflery range. After that we'll have time to catch a fish or two for dinner."

Ted grinned up at his father. "Did you tell *Mutter* we were bringing fish home again?" When Mr. Geisel nodded, Ted suggested, "We could just go to Deesels' Fish Market right away and save time."

Mr. Geisel looked stricken. "Why, Ted!" he said. "Have you no faith in your old *Vater*?"

"Deesels' is the best fishing hole in town, *Vater*. You taught me that." Ted turned back to the workbench. Mr. Geisel pointed to a clamp hanging on the wall. Ted handed it to him, and *Vater* went back to work on a new rack for his gun collection.

Ted looked around the garage. With room for two automobiles and a workbench, it was the envy of all his friends. His last project here had been mousetraps designed not to hurt the mice. He smiled, remembering the fun a loose mouse or two had caused in a classroom. He had made rattles to clatter against neighbors' windows at night, too. How Mrs. Haynes had shrieked! Ted scanned the rows of tools carefully hung in place. The wood scraps and metal pieces were tidy, too. *Vater* insisted they stay that way.

Stilts, he thought. If he were tall enough, he could look right into people's windows. That would be great for Halloween. Ted decided he would practice walking on them all summer. At Halloween, he could dress as a tall monster and scare people in their own homes! He chose two long straight boards and nailed foot pieces to them while his father puttered over the gun rack.

Ted stood up on the stilts and took a few awkward steps. "Look, *Vater*!" he said. His father chuckled and turned back to the workbench. Ted worked to refine the stilts, adding rubber straps. He wound rope around for handholds on the top of each board. All the while, his mind worked on costume ideas to go with the stilts. The stilt monster had to be scary. Very scary.

"I'm done here, son," Mr. Geisel said. Ted leaned his new stilts against the corner of the wall and hurried to wipe off the tools and put each in its place. He swept the workbench corner and tossed the sweepings out. "Good," his father said, cleaning up the last of his own project. "But you missed a place." Ted brushed sawdust off the workbench and into his hand, and then carried that out, too.

"To the Turnverein Club, son?"

"*Vater*?" Ted asked, "Could we visit the zoo first? I have to look at some meat-eaters for costume ideas to go with the stilts."

"I suppose so. It is free now that I'm on their Board of Directors." Mr. Geisel took out his watch and snapped it open. Peering at it, he announced, "We can spend twenty minutes there, no more."

"I'll get my sketchbook!" Ted ran out the door, across the yard, and up the porch steps. He took the staircase three steps at a time. His room was in the back right corner of the house, but he was back downstairs before his father pulled the Hudson 6 around to pick him up.

Ted sat proudly in the front seat. None of his friends had the new six-cylinder automobile. He did not see any of his friends or the scenery, either, in those few blocks, though. His mind was already mixing lions and bears

28

and spiders and snakes to come up with a tall new nightmare.

Vater looked at his watch again as they arrived at the zoo. "Twenty minutes." Ted promised. He hurried to the lion cage and opened his sketchbook.

The lion stretched, yawned, and rose to his feet. It should have looked ferocious. Instead, the lion seemed relaxed. Every joint seemed rubbery; every move a new set of curves. Ted's pencil flew over his sketchpad. As the animal turned again, he started a new sketch. No drawing was quite done, but each caught one piece of the lion's fluid movement.

Now the animal backed up toward a well-clawed stump in the corner of the cage. His tail rose, then twitched as he wet down the wood. The lion's eyes never left the Geisels. The hot, acid scent of cat urine floated from the cage.

"Disgusting," Mr. Geisel said. "We *must* move on."

Ted kept sketching furiously as the cat began to stroll the length of his cage and back. "I love cats," he said quietly. "Look how he watches us with those big yellow eyes. He looks like he is taking notes on us, too."

"I'd rather be doing the watching," Mr. Geisel said. "The ostrich doesn't look back at you like that. The deer don't, either. And I could watch the pheasants all day."

"Fine," said Ted.

"Fine, what?" Mr. Geisel said.

"Let's go watch the pheasants all day."

Mr. Geisel grabbed Ted's cap and swatted him with it. Ted laughed and closed his sketchbook.

They drove to the Turnverein Club downtown. The doorman nodded them in. "*Guten Tag, Herr* Geisel," he said respectfully. Everyone in the club spoke German. *Grossvater* Seuss had helped to found the club years earlier. Fencing lessons, gymnastics, the strange new game called basketball, a swimming pool and more—the Turnverein had everything to develop young German Americans' bodies and minds. Weights, calisthetics, wrestling, boxing, track lessons—all intense, and all taught in German.

"Is my wife here?" Mr. Geisel asked the doorman.

"*Ja, Herr* Geisel. She is at the pool with your little *frauline*." Ted and his father walked by the pool.

Mrs. Geisel waved at them from the top of the high diving board. "Watch this," she called. She took two deep bounces. Then she did a beautiful somersaulting dive, her bathing dress fluttering as she moved. "Not quite top form," she panted after she had swum to the edge. "But it is early in the season yet. I can still win in my class, don't you think?"

"Nettie, you are always a winner."

Ted blinked. It wasn't often he heard his parents speak that way to each other. "Oh, my tender ears!" he cried, shielding them with his hands. *Mutter* splashed water at him and they all laughed.

They said good-bye there, and Ted and his father headed out to the Schützenverein together. The drive was short and the parking lot was almost full. The sound of pistol and rifle shots echoed around the building. The Geisels got their guns out of the back of the car and carried them indoors. "My birthday gun is designed to aim itself, isn't it?" Ted asked.

"*Ja,* and it pulls its own trigger and adds up its own score, too," *Vater* said. The Geisels' stopped laughing when they came to the firing range.

"It's *Herr* Geisel." The word passed from shooter to shooter. The din of a dozen guns firing indoors quickly stilled. One shooter gave up his lane to the club champion.

Everyone was watching as Mr. Geisel took his first six shots at the paper target suspended from a pulley line fifty feet away. It was silent as he reeled the target in. "Six in the center," the whisper went down the line.

"Not bad for a warm-up," *Vater* said. "Now I'm ready for some real shooting." His shots this time were all within the bull's-eye. The next six looked perfect, too. "Your turn, Ted," Mr. Geisel said. As Ted raised his rifle, the coaching began. "Tighten up that leg, Ted. Spread your balance more evenly. Do not anticipate the shot. Is the butt of the rifle snug against your shoulder?" Ted was dizzy by the time his father ran down his list. "Now relax," Mr. Geisel said, "and pull the trigger."

Ted shot. Six times the paper trembled. When they reeled it in, a respectable cluster grouped within the third ring. Mr. Geisel nodded silently.

"Can we go now?" Ted asked.

"Not when you are making such progress. Now is the time to double your efforts."

Ted dutifully reloaded, took aim, and shot. When he retrieved the paper target this time, his shots had landed even farther from the bull's-eye. The next improved, but the fourth round was scattershot.

"I don't understand it," Mr. Geisel said. "You have an excellent eye. You are steady as a rock when you want to be." He slid his rifle into its case. "I had planned to enter team competition with you this year. You're not going to be ready—again."

"Sorry, *Vater*." Ted wished there were something else he could say. The mood of the day was gone. He followed his father toward the lockers. "Do you want to go fishing, *Vater*?"

Mr. Geisel drove in silence to their normal parking space at Forest Park. They carried poles and gear to the shore of the lake. The waterway twisted and turned through the city park and was bordered by broad lawns and deep groves of trees. Everywhere, Springfielders took in the sun of a lovely Saturday afternoon. Little children tossed breadcrumbs to greedy ducks. Older children climbed and swung on playground equipment nearby. Young women in daringly short skirts showed off their ankles. They sported short hair and rouged cheeks, too. Ted was glad Marnie had more sense. Sweethearts strolled in pairs, hands nearly touching. The Geisels hurried past everyone to their favorite fishing hole.

They cast without a word. And waited. They cast again, staring at bobbins frozen in silence. Ted had no words to say to his father. He'd had no idea they were supposed to compete together this year. The bobbins lay perfectly still on the water's surface. There were no fish out there. Ted felt sure of it. *Vater* glared at the water. Ted felt the tension rise until he thought *Vater* would explode with frustration.

Suddenly Ted knew what to do. He tried not to giggle as he made his pole twitch. The bobbin followed suit. "I think I have something, *Vater*!" he said, springing to his feet. He pretended to haul mightily at a giant catch. He swung the pole wildly and grunted

36

with imagined effort. Mr. Geisel smiled at him. "It's a bass and a half!" Ted cried. A moment later he announced, "No, it's a shark. A great killem up park shark!"

"Shall I hold back small children?" Mr. Geisel asked.

"No, save yourself!" Ted groaned, backing up the bank. "It's a giant whale, hungry for lunch. German sausage in particular."

Mr. Giesel was laughing aloud now. "Fine. Reel in this catch, Teddy, and we will head over to Deesels' Fish Market. Your mother will never know the difference."

Ted was still grinning as they swaggered into Deesels'. His joke had saved the day!

"Let me guess," Mr. Deesel said. He stared at the Geisels from behind the counter of his fish store. "Trout again. Three or four—of a believable size."

Ted and his father looked at each other. "Six," Mr. Geisel said. "Or make it seven. The two of us did very well today."

The Hun

At first, Ted could ignore it, or pretend it did not matter. It seemed like any schoolyard teasing. The German Americans had never been close to the English families anyway— or the Italians, the Swedes, or the Poles. And no one spoke with the black kids. You never saw them. Negroes had their own schools. They sat in their own section of the theaters and buses. That was how it was in 1914. As far as Ted knew, that was how it had always been. Everybody at school got along, more or less.

They teased each other, of course. There were rude names for the other groups, and jokes—dozens of them. It was easy to make fun of other people, but that was all it was—fun. That was all it had seemed, until lately.

"Marnie, what do you do when they make fun of you?" Ted asked.

His sister did not have to ask what he meant. Things were bad at the high school, too.

"Let's get out of here," Marnie said. "Tennis at Forest Park again?"

Ted nodded. "I'll beat the pants off you! Anything's better than sitting at home, listening to the arguments." The government of Germany, their "homeland," had turned aggressive. Its powerful army was threatening neighboring countries. Some of the Geisels' German relatives were proud of their government. Others were horrified.

Ted's family saw their homeland for what it was—a threat to world peace. The Kaiser,

Germany's ruler, was threatening to attack other nations. No one had struck at them, but they had a strong army and believed it was their right. People began to distrust Germans, and German Americans, too.

"Get out, you dirty Hun." "Germans are mean as Atilla the Hun." "Go home where you belong." "No German Huns Allowed." The hateful signs the Geisels saw every day on the way to school hurt. Even worse, classmates began to whisper about them. They stopped inviting them to parties. It got harder to make new friends. Old friends pulled away from German Americans, in case they were like the Kaiser.

Marnie and Ted spent more time together. They stayed at home instead of facing the growing anti-German prejudice. Marnie studied and practiced piano. Ted read the funny papers and drew.

Krazy Kat was the nation's favorite comic strip. Ted copied the Kat, but he changed it, too. The loose, curving shapes of the Forest Park lion crept into his drawings. He whimsically mixed animal parts the way Ian Blackwood did in *The Bad Child's Book of Beasts* and other books. He played with the silly humor, too, imitating it in his own jokes.

"Things are changing," Mrs. Geisel said one night at supper. It was 1915. "The Seuss Bakery's business is dropping off. What if my father has to close the business? I'm worried about him."

Marnie spread butter on a thick slice of pumpernickel bread so rich it was almost black. "What's wrong with the bakery?"

"Nothing," *Mutter* said. "And I don't want to worry you. People just aren't buying the ryes and dark breads like they used to."

"Not when the bakery name is 'Seuss,'" Mr. Geisel said. "It's not the flavor; it's the nation behind the name. Germany. The brewery is suffering, too."

"It is?" This was news to Ted.

"Customers just aren't ordering German beer like they used to," Mr. Geisel said slowly. "Even if it is named 'Liberty,' they say Huns made it."

"That's not fair!" Marnie exploded. "They're even taking the German language books off the library shelves. I need those books for school!" Marnie took a big breath. "We don't have anything to do with what Germany is doing—but we get punished for it just because of some great-great-*Grossvater* I never met and don't give a hoot about."

Marnie blushed wildly after her outburst. Mr. Geisel looked angry enough to hurt someone. *Mutter* seemed about to cry. Ted looked at the half-eaten knockwurst on his plate, wishing he could melt away. Things were too bad for a joke now. Nobody was laughing at his pranks, either. There was not a thing he could say to make things better. Nobody could.

A dreadful question hung unspoken in the

air. What if our country goes to war with our Homeland? It was so bad now for them in Springfield. What if it got worse?

The anti-German mood was not the Geisels' only worry.

People were beginning to agree with Mrs. Haynes and the women who marched demanding an end to sales of liquor and beer. "Alcohol wrecks families," the Temperance League argued. "It should be prohibited." Everyone knew of at least one family ruined by alcoholism, so their words seemed true.

"Alcohol takes money from the poor and gives it to the rich," the League claimed. Everyone remembered seeing a drunken homeless man passed out on a park bench. They had also seen the flashy beer wagons making their deliveries. It was hard to argue with the logic. Alcohol sometimes caused terrible problems.

One day Ted walked past a small group of women standing on the street corner. They were reading a piece of paper. One of them caught his eye and smiled. Few people had been friendly to Ted lately. He tipped his cap. Ted felt a stiffness leave his shoulders as he grinned at her. "Will you sign the Pledge?" she asked. Her voice was warm and encouraging.

"To be loyal to America?" he asked. "Of course I'll sign! I'm an American first and forever!" That would solve everything, he thought.

"No," she said, laughing. "Silly boy. I want you to pledge to give up alcohol forever."

An older woman glanced over. "Elizabeth!" she hissed. Don't you know who that *is*?" All the women were looking at him now.

"That's a *Geisel*!" one woman said. She made it sound like a dirty thing. "His family owns the Liberty Brewering Company."

Elizabeth tossed her head and turned away, but not before Ted saw the disgust in her eyes. "You make the devil's brew," a gray-haired woman told him. "You spread disease and death among the poor. How can you live with yourself?"

Ted felt his mouth drop open. No words came out.

"You know," Elizabeth said, turning back to look at him, "if he *did* take the Pledge, it would be a wonderful thing. Imagine the headline: *Beer maker's son rejects beer.* That would be so good for the cause!" She smiled broadly at Ted and offered him the paper and a pen.

Ted turned on his heel and stormed away.

No matter how funny Ted tried to make it sound that night at the dinner table, nobody laughed.

"Those prohibitionists are so certain they are right," *Mutter* sputtered. "Self-righteous people are thoughtless and bossy. I just ignore them."

"A lot of Americans are taking the Pledge." *Vater's* voice sounded tired.

"At school, they're called teetotalers," Marnie said. "Those prohibitionists swear they'll drink nothing stronger than tea. I hate them."

"You heard the minister on Sunday," *Vater* said. "Churches are getting behind the movement. Politicians in Washington, too. It might even become law."

"I'll drink to that. Pass the beer!" Ted said. It was the only funny thing he could think of. He'd been trying to be funny since things had turned bad. His friends at school thought he was hilarious. The teachers, the neighbors, and, normally, his own family loved his witty remarks. Tonight, nobody at the Geisel house was laughing.

That night the Geisels gathered in the music room to listen to the radio. They expected the static. They expected a short news program, then a radio play. They did not expect the announcer to tell them, "Congress has passed an eighteenth amendment to the

Constitution prohibiting the sale of alcohol."

"What!" Marnie jumped up. "They can't do that! We're ruined!"

"Prohibition?" *Mutter* said. She covered her face with her hands.

Mr. Geisel snapped the radio off. In the sudden silence, he said, "Never. It will never happen. Three-quarters of the states have to vote for it. That process alone will take months and months. This temperance movement is just a fad. It will fade long before they get the votes to put it in the Constitution."

He stormed out of the room and slammed the door shut.

Later that night, Ted heard angry voices coming from downstairs. He snuck out to sit on the top step. It was his father and his uncle, sitting on the bottom step. They were passing a bottle of whiskey between them and it was almost empty.

"Y'know," Mr. Geisel slurred. "Best thing

we could do is deliver a keg to the Haynes household. Right in broad daylight."

"Pass that bottle back," Uncle Will said. "Better yet, do that and add a note saying the beer is a gift from her best friend in the Temperance Club. What is that cow's name?"

"Bumps," Mr. Geisel said. "Mrs. Bumps. And don't you think we should send a keg to Mrs. Bumps, too? From Mrs. Haynes?" The men sat on the step rocking with laughter until the moon came up.

Ted crept off to bed thinking the plan was a good one. The next day nothing was said of it—and it was never mentioned again.

Many other things were said that year, most of them unkind.

Mrs. Geisel's eyes filled with tears as she reported a comment she had overheard in the market: "There's the woman," a gossipy neighbor had said, pointing at her. "Her husband sells Geisel beer to alcoholics so they are too poor to buy Seuss bread for their children."

The annual gymnastics exhibition by the children of the Turnverein Club had long been famous in Springfield. This year hardly anyone came to watch the children's hard work.

In the Fourth of July parade, more women marched under the Temperance banners than for the right to vote. The Geisel family stood on the curb waving American flags at the floats and bands, the soldiers and the Scouts. When the Prohibitionists passed the Geisels, most of the women hissed loudly. The others turned their faces away.

Ted wanted to throw a rock at them. He wanted to rip their banners down. He wanted to get those self-righteous women back for hurting his family.

There was nothing he could do but glare. Ted promised himself he would settle the injustice someday. In the meantime, he found

a way to overcome the prejudice. He sharpened his pencils and drew cartoons. He honed his wit and cracked jokes all the time. Ted became the class clown at school. He was the class comic, too, in junior high. It was a lot of work to keep his spirits up and act playful all the time. He had to keep thinking of more jokes and puns than ever before.

No matter how tired, hurt, angry, or bored he was, Ted was always ready with a smile and a quip. His practical jokes became a legend in school. It all paid off. He might have been a German American whose father made the "devil's brew," but Ted Geisel had made himself popular.

Liberty Bonds

Ted entered Central High School in eighth grade, determined to make his mark. Marnie was one of the school's top students. "We expect great things of you, too, Theodor," the teachers predicted, seeing another Geisel in their classroom.

Ted was not so sure. Central was the Springfield school for students who planned to go to college. Ted knew Central classes were tough. He did not like studying. Ted was not interested in Central's sports teams, either. But there was a school newspaper that had funny articles sometimes, and cartoons. That sounded like a place where Ted's talent could shine. He stopped by the *Central Recorder* room and dropped off a few cartoons and lots of jokes in the first weeks of school.

Several of them were printed in the *Recorder* the very next month. More important to Ted, his writing was accepted, too. He loved seeing his words in print. He also loved knowing how many of the students were reading his work. They published his one-line jokes. He wrote a paragraph for them each week, signed "Pete the Pessimist." He wrote essays, poetry, and news articles. Some were funny. Others were not. Ted decided he would be a brewery president *and* a writer.

One by one, states across the country were voting in favor of the Eighteenth Amendment. No one knew whether it would finally become part of the Constitution, so Ted and his family ignored it. Like most people from European cultures, the Geisels let their children drink beer and wine. These were not special party drinks to them. They were just something served with meals. Ted didn't think about it as he wrote for the newspaper.

He wrote so much that he used pseudonyms in the paper instead of his real name. That way it did not look like one student was taking up too much space. "Pete the Pessimist" was just one of the names he used. Ted was not really a pessimist, expecting the worst to happen. He was much more like the cheery "Ole the Optimist," another of his many pseudonyms. Sometimes he wrote as "TSG," "Theodor Geisel," "T.G.," or "Ted." He sometimes even turned his name backward and spelled it "LeSieg."

His father used that name in secret. "What if you get caught at your betting?" Mrs. Geisel had said. "You'll ruin our reputation if you bet using the Geisel name. And don't you dare think to use Seuss, either!" So Mr. Geisel had gone on betting, pretending to be "Mr. LeSieg."

Mr. Geisel wanted Ted to play on a sports team in high school. Instead, Ted was manager of the high school soccer club. They lost every game. His father insisted he take fencing lessons, gymnastics, and even ballroom dance classes at the Turnverein Sports Club. Ted attended each, just to make his father happy.

Mr. Geisel was upset most of the time now. A dozen European countries were allied in a coalition, fighting against Germany and its allies. Some Americans wanted to help their friends. Others wanted to stay out of the fight. Arguments flared as the Kaiser's troops moved into France. They had already invaded Poland and other European countries. When America sent Navy ships full of relief supplies, Germany attacked them. They even torpedoed a British cruise ship, the *Lusitania*. Over a thousand people died, including 128 Americans. Finally, on April 6, 1917, the United States declared war against Germany.

"Listen to this," Mr. Geisel said. His voice shook as he read the paper to his family. "Berlin, Iowa, has changed its name to 'Lincoln.' The government has dissolved the German-American Alliance—even our local club. In some cities German Americans have been beaten."

"It is getting silly, too," Ted said. "Congress has announced that sauerkraut must now be called 'liberty cabbage' and frankfurters will be 'hot dogs.'"

"What about German shepherd dogs?" Marnie asked. "May we say *that*?"

"Of course not. They are now 'Alsatians,'" Ted said, laughing.

"This isn't funny, children," Mrs. Geisel said. "Forty-seven members of our Turnverein Club volunteered for the Army in one day. You know them all. They are going overseas to fight against our homeland." There were tears in her eyes.

There were tears in many homes. Thousands upon thousands of troops left America for battle. Factories stayed open extra hours to make supplies for them all. The soldiers had to be fed, too. Ordinary Americans threw themselves into helping with the war effort.

Ted's Boy Scout troop learned skills to help defend the country. Troop 13 practiced marching in uniform until they looked as smart as any army unit. They learned how to read maps and plot a course by compass at night. Ted already knew how to shoot. Now he learned flag signals and Morse code, first aid, swimming, lifesaving skills, and emergency crowd control. He was ready in case the German army invaded the United Sates.

"Can I sell you some Liberty Bonds?" he asked everyone. Troop 13 was having a contest to see who could sell the most bonds.

These were like savings bonds, but all the money went to help buy rifles and build ships. Ted sold at the brewery, the bakery, the Turnverein, and the riflery club, too. *Grossvater* Geisel bought a thousand dollars worth. People everywhere were glad to buy the bonds to support the war. Ted was one of the top ten sellers.

He was excited when he heard about the big award ceremony. "What do you mean, Theodore Roosevelt is going to thank you?" *Vater* asked. Ted explained that the former president was going to present medals to the top-selling Boy Scouts. The entire Geisel and Seuss families turned out at the Municipal Auditorium. On the stage, Ted stood proud in his Scout uniform. He was last in the line. Ted waved nervously at his family in the seats below. *Mutter* wiped her eyes with a handkerchief and Ted looked away. One by one, the boys heard their names called. Each walked up to the president and saluted.

Roosevelt handed each a medal. He thanked them and shook their hands.

"Theodor Seuss Geisel." Ted heard the scoutmaster call his name. He walked toward the old president, but something was wrong. Roosevelt was looking at the scoutmaster. His hands were empty. The scoutmaster was shrugging.

Roosevelt stared at Ted. "What's this little boy doing here?" he said loudly. The scoutmaster frowned and hurried Ted offstage.

In the dark behind the curtain, Ted fought tears. "What did I do wrong? Is it because I'm German?" he asked. "Is it because of my *Vater's* brewery?"

"No, no. Nothing like that. I just miscounted the medals," the scoutmaster explained. "I can't understand how I did that." Ted was silent. In front of thousands of people, he had been called a "little boy" and sent away. He was fourteen. A high school student. Waves of embarrassment rolled over

59

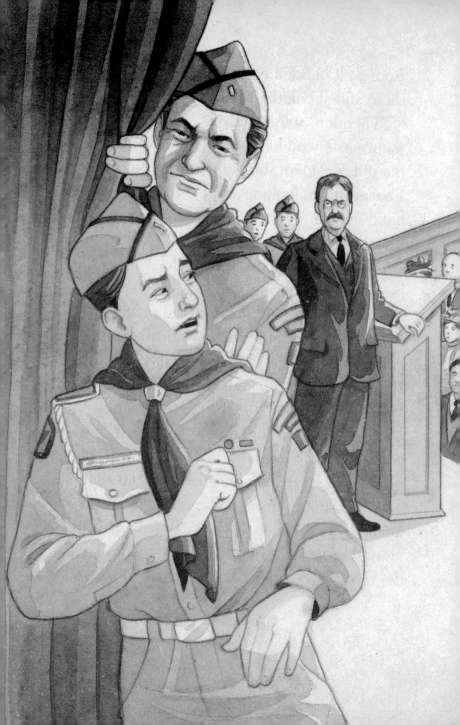

him. Then his anger began to rise. How could this happen to him?

"Well," the scoutmaster said briskly. "We'll get you a medal later." Ted did not dare to speak. He was too furious to control what he might say. "Never mind, then," the scoutmaster said. "You still have the satisfaction of knowing you helped our boys over there."

Everyone pitched in to help "our boys." To help gather metal for ships and helmets, Ted saved tinfoil. He collected rubber bands for factories to make into tires for the soldiers. Over the summer, he grew a "Victory Garden" in his yard in Springfield. The idea was to help feed his own family so the farmer's crops could go straight to "our boys." Anne baked Victory Bread, made of gritty whole grains. That saved the fine-ground white flour for shipment overseas. Marnie and *Mutter* knit bandages and warm socks for the soldiers.

They learned the war news at night, as the

family gathered around the radio in the music room. Now they could also see some of the news at the movie theaters. Suddenly movies had sound. It was a magic change, and Ted fell in love with movies.

Ted did not love school. His least favorite class was Latin. Since that class was at the end of the day, he often cut school. He would sneak downtown for a show. Sometimes he went to movie theaters. Other times he went to see live plays on stage.

Plays held more magic for him than movies. The theater owners saw Ted so often that they got to know the funny young man, and they liked him. By summertime, they gave Ted a job at the Court Square Theater. Before every play he ushered people to their seats. Just as the lights went down, he found a place for himself to sit and watch for free.

Ted could not invite dates to these shows. Instead, he asked them out for canoe rides.

"Ted might benefit from the workout of paddling a canoe," the coach at the Turnverein had told Mr. Geisel. *Vater* bought Ted a canoe, hoping his son would finally enjoy a sport. Ted took friends and girlfriends out for picnics and parties on the lake in Forest Park all summer. It did not help his muscles much, but it was great for his social life.

In September, all social life came to a sudden end. The strange "Spanish Flu" struck Springfield. Some of its victims died within hours. Others were sick for weeks. It spread like wildfire. Soon Springfield's hospitals were full. The funeral parlors were busy night and day. "It is everywhere," *Vater* said, looking up from the newspaper. "This sickness is sweeping the globe."

Ted's theater closed. At Central High, he had to wear a face mask of white cotton. The teachers, the principal, the nurse, the janitor, and the crossing guards wore them, too.

When masks did not slow the epidemic, school was closed.

For nearly a month, Ted and Marnie stayed home with *Mutter*, away from crowds. There was nowhere else to go, anyhow. The Turnverein, the rifle range, the zoo, and the park were closed down.

Then, just as suddenly as it had started, the epidemic ended. Hundreds of thousands of people had died. Thousands more were left worn out and weak. Many desks stood empty in the classrooms when Ted went back to school. It was a sad October. Marnie's best friend had died. Ted had lost two of his teachers. Six times more Americans died in the flu epidemic of 1918 than in all of the war's battles put together.

The country needed good news—and it got it. The war ended on November 11 at 11:11 in the morning, with the signing of a treaty.

When the announcement came across the radio, the Geisels headed out into the streets.

They screamed and cried with relief. No more young men would die. The German Americans would be accepted again. *Vater* drank and danced with *Mutter*. Firecrackers and fire sirens went off. Local bands gathered to play patriotic tunes on street corners. All of Springfield was a party. Beer and whiskey flowed everywhere. State by state, prohibition was passing into law, but nobody wanted to be a teetotaler at a time like this.

"Let's raise a glass," Mr. Geisel said at the family table that night. The whole family stood and held their beers high. For a moment, Mr. Geisel was too emotional to speak. Everyone had time to think about what toast they would offer. For the German Americans to get back the respect they had once had? For the soldiers to come home safely? For world peace after what everyone was calling "the war to end all wars?"

Mutter spoke aloud. "Here's to our family, alive and well after all of this."

"Here! Here!" they said, and "Cheers." They clinked their glasses together.

Now the parades began. Within hours, Springfield was planning the biggest victory celebration its people had ever seen. Fireworks were shot off every night over the Connecticut River. Parades welcomed home the troops as they returned from Europe. Concerts and speeches honored them. Springfield dedicated new statues and memorials to their fallen soldiers. That was sad, but the mood in the country was overwhelming relief.

With the war, the epidemic, and the parties over, Ted just looked forward to getting back to a normal life.

The Minstrel Show

"We will draw this," the art teacher said, handing out charcoal and great white sheets of paper. Ted sat staring at a bunch of wilted daisies in an old milk bottle. His shoulders slumped. This was not what he had expected from his first high school art class. "What would a cow do?" he whispered to his classmates. "Eat the daisies or squirt milk on them?" Laughter rippled around him, as he knew it would.

"Silence," the art teacher said, and the giggles stopped.

Ted began sketching the daisies. He turned his paper around to sketch the milk bottle beneath them. With the drawing upside down, he could see that the shadows under the daisies needed to be darker. He was working on that when the teacher strolled by.

"Exactly what do you think you are doing?" she asked.

"Drawing." Ted said. He went on working as giggles spread again.

"Young man," the teacher said. "Turn your paper around this minute." Ted looked at her in disbelief. The new perspective had really helped his work. His still life was looking better than any of the other drawings in class. He went back to work.

"No, Theodor," the teacher said, loud enough that everyone in the classroom heard. "*Not* upside down! There are rules that every artist must abide by. You will never succeed if you break them."

Ted sat frozen. This was not fair. And it was

not right. Rulebooks did not govern art. He waited until the hour was over before he went to the principal's office and signed out of the class. "I'll never take another art course," he said.

Other teachers at Central could work with Ted's wildly creative streak. "Ted, you have a gift," his English teacher said after class one day.

"Why? It's not my birthday!" Ted joked back.

"I don't mean your wit," Mr. Smith said. "I think you have what it takes to be a writer." His voice was so serious that Ted stopped teasing. He was startled and excited that an adult believed in his talent—and his future. Ted worked with Mr. Smith on the newspaper and took every class he could with this dynamic teacher. Mr. Smith shared Ted's love of playful poetry. They recited funny poems together. Mr. Smith urged Ted to experiment with words in poetry. "Play with other kinds of writing, too."

"Call me Red," Mr. Smith said one day.

That was a great leap in friendship at a time when students never called teachers by their first names. Red was not just a teacher and a friend. He was Ted's cheerleader, too.

"This is great," he often said as he handed back Ted's papers. "Now let's see if we can make it even better." He encouraged Ted from the beginning. "Submit your work. This is good enough to be in the school newspaper." "Try something different." "Play with your words."

Sometimes, Ted's work was rejected by the school paper. "I'm just not sure I'm good enough," he admitted. Red was the only one who heard this kind of talk from flashy, popular Teddy Geisel.

"This happens to all writers," Red would say. "Remember, they didn't reject *you*. They just don't want this one piece of writing. Send them something else and keep sending until your work is accepted."

Ted learned this lesson well. By his junior year, the *Central Recorder* made him a staff member. It was an outlet for his writing and illustrations—and for his wit.

He was still working at the Court Square Theater, too. Watching the plays fed his lively imagination. He began to appear in plays at school. First, he held a comic role in *The Mikado*. Later, Ted was hilarious as one of the characters in Shakespeare's *Twelfth Night*. But in or out of plays, Ted seemed always to be onstage. Classmates marveled at his energy as they chuckled or groaned at his jokes.

For one assignment, he wrote his own play. It was funny, of course. "This is good enough to present to the whole school, and parents, too," the theater coach told him. "Let's present it this spring." Ted directed it. He designed the scenery. He appeared only as a mandolin player onstage, but he was able to watch the effects of his words on a large audience. There was such power in them. Some of his words made people boo. Some of the writing made people chuckle quietly, while other parts made them laugh aloud. A few times the crowd seemed bored. Ted thought how he might have changed the script to keep them interested. At the end, they stood and roared with laughter—and applause.

Besides working onstage and writing for the newspaper, Ted started a mandolin club and performed with them. He told jokes between classical numbers. He played in the school's jazz band, too. He honed his speech in the debating club. Ted was everywhere at school—except on the sports field.

Gradually, his father became proud of his nonathletic son. *Mutter* attended every performance and concert. Marnie did too, until she graduated from high school. She got top honors. Smith College, right up the Connecticut River from Springfield, invited her to study there. The family still gathered in the music room to play their instruments and sing together. There they relaxed and listened to the radio.

The news was bad for the Geisel family. State

after state voted to make alcohol illegal. The Temperance movement was winning. At last, they heard the official announcement: The Eighteenth Amendment had become law. A nationwide prohibition on liquor would begin a year later. The beer industry was doomed.

"Will you close the brewery now?" Ted asked.

"Absolutely not," *Vater* said. "We have a year left until this madness takes effect. We will keep making and delivering the best beers in the world to our customers."

It was a grim year for the Geisels.

In the fall, *Grossvater* Geisel died. There was little time for sorrow. Ted's father was the new president of the brewery business. A few weeks later, his product became illegal. He had to shut the brewery down. He had to fire hundreds of dedicated workers and longtime friends. There were brewery plants to shut down in other cities, too. Mr. Geisel did not spend much time with his family that winter.

Mutter and Marnie were watching another constitutional amendment win passage in state after state. Men were voting to allow women the right to vote. Marnie hugged her mother. "Soon," she promised. "We'll go to the polls and vote together!"

"Just you wait," Mrs. Geisel said to her husband. "Things will be different when women have their say!"

"You will vote as I tell you," Mr. Geisel said flatly.

"Yes, dear," Mrs. Geisel said in a very meek voice. "Of course, dear." Mrs. Geisel and Marnie smiled at each other. Men voted in secret ballots, they both knew. The women would, too. *Vater* would never know how they had used their new power. Ted caught Marnie's eye and winked.

"The whole country is going to the dogs," Mr. Geisel said. He picked up his stein and took a long swig of beer.

Women got the right to vote on August 26,

1920. Within weeks, Ted was back at Central for his senior year. He became one of the editors of the school newspaper. Ted's secret dream was to become an English teacher like Red. He even wondered about being a professor of English. Ted knew whom to ask about college.

"You know that I went to Dartmouth," Red said. He told Ted about the school tucked in the New Hampshire mountains. "I think you'd like it there. Moreover, I think it would be very good for your writing. Whatever you do, you must use that gift," Red urged. "I'll write to some of my friends at Dartmouth. Your grades might not be the best, but when they hear about your talent . . ."

Ted used all of his gifts to help his class. It had been hard to raise money during the war years. The seniors did not have enough money to take their class trip to Washington, D.C. "Let's do one last show to raise the rest of the money," Ted suggested to his friends.

"We'll make it an old-fashioned minstrel show. Most of us sing or play instruments, right? This would be one last chance to perform for each other." Ted's voice rose with enthusiasm. "All of our parents would come, too. And they would pay."

"I bet we could get the winners of the dance competition to perform," someone said. Then the ideas came fast. "Isn't there a junior who juggles? He'd love to show off." "We could do spoofs of the teachers." "Or maybe some of them would perform?" One of the students knew that her teacher sang at the theater. "She'd do it," she said. "Our class would go down in Central High history!"

"But who would direct the whole thing?" someone asked. They all looked at Ted.

He grinned, shuffled his feet, and said, "Aw, shucks, folks." Everyone laughed and the group split up to search out talents for the show.

The end of the year passed in a blur for Ted. He was on the prom committee. He was one of the captains of the debate team. He was an editor for the *Central Reporter*. He performed in the final concerts of the school jazz band, too.

Ted loved the creative frenzy of his life. Besides everything else, he handled all the details for the fundraiser and he was its announcer, too. He also performed in it. He sang two solo songs in his clear, warm voice. He played his instruments. He told jokes.

Ted had discovered that people thought he was funnier if he delivered his jokes without a smile. The surprise of this "dry" wit made them laugh even harder. They never knew from his face when he was pulling their leg or spinning another impossible story. In photographs, he looked very serious. In life, he was hilarious.

The class trip to Washington was a huge success. Ted finally shook a president's hand. President Warren Harding received the class in the Capitol's rotunda, and this time everything went smoothly for Ted.

Vater was not there to see it, though. He was home, trying to settle his father's estate. He was also looking for a job. None of his business contacts could help him. Bars had closed and restaurants were laying off employees, too. It seemed people would not eat as much or spend money the way they had before Prohibition. Luckily, Mr. Geisel had other things to celebrate.

Ted had been accepted to Dartmouth. Although Ted did not bring home sports trophies, *Vater* was proud of his son's achievements. The students voted Ted "class wit." Even though he had never taken an art course, he was "class artist," too. There were no academic honors in Ted's record, but he marched with dozens of good friends in the graduation ceremony. As he got his diploma, the applause was loud and long. Everyone knew Theodor Geisel, and everyone loved him.

Ted thought college could only be better.

Jack-O-Lantern

Dartmouth College was a four-hour train trip north from Springfield. Ted's parents and sister came up to Hanover, New Hampshire, with him the first time. They rented a taxi to take them to the campus and saw him settled into his dorm room.

"I'm glad you brought Theophrastus," *Mutter* said. She looked at the bed and patted the old toy dog on its head. "He'll always take care of you." Her eyes filled up with tears. "Write often, son, please?"

"Not fair," Marnie said. "Your room is so

much bigger than mine at Smith, and you have this one all to yourself." She stood gazing out from the fourth floor window at all the lawns and walkways. "There's another difference out there. Just look at all those *men*."

"Quick, Henrietta, cover her eyes!" Mr. Geisel said. The whole family laughed. There were no boys at Marnie's school and no girls at Ted's. The laughter trailed off. It was time to say good-bye.

Hundreds of new students and their families stood on the green hugging or stiffly shaking hands. They had come from all over the country, and most were away from home for the first time. The good-byes took hours. At last the boys wandered back to their rooms.

Ted knew just what to do: learn people's names and use them often. It was a trick for making friends fast. Ted introduced himself to everyone. One of the older boys, "L." Bonner, told him, "I'm on the staff of the school magazine, the *Jack-O-Lantern*."

"Do they print cartoons?" Ted asked.

"Well, it *is* a humor magazine. I'm only involved in the literary end of things," Bonner admitted, "but, yes, we can always use a cartoonist. You any good?"

Ted went to work. He drew dozens of cartoons of freshmen, of the campus, of puns, and of the politics of 1921. They included strange animals and knowing, smiling cats. He spread them out on his bed next to his stuffed toy dog, Theophrastus. He picked out the best of them. Then Bonner walked him to the busy *Jack-O-Lantern* office and introduced him around.

Ted handed his work to the artistic editor. "Say, these are good!" the boy said. He glanced at them and handed them back. Ted grinned. "We might be able to use you someday. Drop them over there. And leave your name somewhere." Ted nodded but the student had gone back to work. Ted felt his smile wilt. Everyone in the cluttered office was older than him. Ted was used to being the senior that everyone at the high school knew. He left the office discouraged.

That was not his only disappointment. Some of the most popular clubs at Dartmouth were fraternities. They had secret handshakes, ceremonies, and oaths. Not everyone could join. In the fall, fraternity brothers chose to invite only those new students they wanted in their clubs.

Not one fraternity sent Ted an invitation. He could not understand it. Everyone had loved him at Central High School. Why was he being excluded here? He had not done anything wrong! It was almost like the worst days of German-American hatred in Springfield.

Weeks later, a classmate asked him something about being Jewish. When Ted said he was not a Jew, the boy was stunned. "But everyone thought, with your dark hair and eyes, and that nose . . ."

It was too cruel to be true. The fraternities

had rejected him because they thought he was Jewish—and they did not want Jews. That wasn't fair. He was the victim of prejudice again. It made him furious—and it made him think. This was not happening just to him. Discrimination stung many people. He tried to think of other groups that suffered like this. The Polish? He had heard many Polish jokes. Negroes? He flinched. Dartmouth freshmen? They had been the butt of everyone's jokes. Even one of Ted's comics for the *Jack-O-Lantern* had made fun of freshmen. He'd used this cruel kind of humor to get laughs many times.

Ted decided to stop being such a bigot. He spent a bitter weekend alone in his room, thinking. Soon Ted began looking for another way to make his mark at Dartmouth. He wanted a place where his talents counted, not his class or skin color, religion or national background.

Dartmouth College had a book for freshmen

called the *Green Book* that published pictures of all 525 new students and told a little bit about each of them. Ted tried out by submitting some writing and a few cartoons. None of them used prejudice to get a laugh. As a result, he was invited to be one of the art editors. He also ran for treasurer of the freshman class. He wanted to win, so he made a point of being funny and friendly with the boys in his class. Ted talked about his minstrel show and all the money it had made. He was always ready to sing a number from the show or tell some of the naughtier jokes. He won the election.

Ted also had to attend classes and study. Dartmouth was a men's school, so there were no girls around during the day to distract him. There were clubs nearby, though. Ted began to show up late at night at Scotty's. The place was an easy walk from the college and it offered cheap food, so many students hung out there. Girls from downtown Hanover, New Hampshire, showed up there to meet the Dartmouth men, dance, and eat. The place was lively night after night. They broke the law by selling beer and liquor.

Many places did, but always in secret. The police could arrest anyone who was drinking alcohol and anyone who sold drinks, too. Millions of people were angry about prohibition. They made their own beer, wine, or liquor in backyards or even in bathtubs. A secret black market formed to transport liquor to clubs and stores. They snuck it to Scotty's. Scotty's sold it to Ted.

Ted was as busy—and as happy—as he had been in high school. When the first edition of the *Jack-O-Lantern* came out, late in September, Ted only glanced through it. Suddenly he stopped flipping the pages. There was his cat cartoon! He went back and looked more closely. *Four* of his pieces appeared in the paper. "We want more of your work," Bonner told him.

Ted submitted a few more pieces that year,

but he was too busy to do any more. The freshmen *Green Book* took a lot of his time. The year was a great success in everything but grades. The next year, Mr. Geisel sent him off with an urgent message. "I still haven't found a new job. Money is tight. Paying for college is getting harder, so you'd better not waste a minute of it."

Ted tried to buckle down. He signed up for English classes, business, and science, too. He even signed up for a class in advertising. He thought that mix should make his father happy, since it could lead to lots of different high-paying jobs someday. His secure future as a brewer had vanished.

It was his work at *Jacko* that made Ted happy. That year he was on the *Jack-O-Lantern* staff, and his work appeared in every issue. He spent more nights at the cluttered office than he did at Scotty's. One morning, they found him fast asleep, his face cradled on the typewriter keys.

He got to know the staff of *The Dartmouth,* too. The boys on the college newspaper were as creative and driven as the *Jacko* crowd. They all had deadlines and English classes and high spirits in common. They often played poker together. Everybody knew about their crazy jokes and adventures. After one wild night, Ted confided to Whitney Campbell that he intended to be the editor-in-chief of the *Jack-O-Lantern* by senior year. "Well, that's something!" Whitney said. "*I* plan to be the editor-in-chief of *The Dartmouth* senior year." They toasted the vow with beer.

Ted and Whit became lifelong friends as they went after their dual goals. It took endless hours in their offices. They took extra English courses to hone their skills and edited each other's work. There were lots of politics involved with becoming editor. It meant making friends with the right upperclassmen. They had to impress the right professors and advisors. There were important golf games and polite receptions to attend. Ted and Whit laughed about them afterward, but they never lost sight of their goals. They met countless newspaper deadlines. Classwork had to come second, and their grades showed it.

At the end of junior year, both Ted and Whit heard good news. They would be editors for the next year.

As senior year began, Ted made some changes at the *Jack-O-Lantern*. It was still raucous and witty, but it did not poke fun at the freshmen. There were no cruel jokes about newcomers or jokes about minorities on campus. There were, of course, plenty of puns and cartoons and winking jokes about the "devil's brew."

Both Ted and Whit joined the Casque and Gauntlet. That was an honorary club of only twenty Dartmouth men. The graduating seniors chose their replacements from among the most popular, successful, and important juniors. Whit went to live in the society's castlelike house. Ted could not afford it. He stayed in his cheap apartment where he could still pay for a party or two.

Everyone wanted to be at Ted's and Whit's parties. Ted always brought laughter to a crowd, and he often brought liquor, too. One night, a month before graduation, one of their parties got too loud. The apartment owner called the police. The cops snuck up to the door, then stormed in. They arrested everyone for illegal possession of alcohol. Ted spent the night in jail.

The president of the University had to be called in. Most of his top senior students were involved. The university president and the chief of police struck a deal. The students were returned to campus. They had to write to their parents and confess everything. They could finish their year and graduate, but with a big difference. The students lost any club position or office they had held.

Ted and Whit were out of the Casque and Gauntlet. Worse, Whit was no longer editor-in-chief of *The Dartmouth*. And Ted had no place at the *Jack-O-Lantern*. The boys were stunned. They had lived every moment of their college careers to get those editorial positions.

It was a dismal last month of college. Mr. Geisel wrote back to his son after he got the letter about drinking. He wasn't so upset by that, of course. He had never agreed with prohibition. "But what *are* you planning to do next year?" he asked pointedly. "Marnie went to graduate school, you know. Other neighbors' children have gone on to become lawyers or doctors. What are *your* plans?"

Ted chewed on his pencil before he wrote back. Several of his friends had gotten scholarships to study at Oxford College in England. It had not seemed too hard to get the money award to go. Besides, there was no Prohibition in England.

"Dear *Vater*," he wrote. "You will be happy to know I am applying for a scholarship to study at Oxford. In two years, I will return and be a professor of English."

"Mein Gott!" Mr. Geisel shouted as soon as he read the letter. "Come, Henrietta, come quick! Our boy is going to school in England!"

He read the letter aloud to his wife. Without even pausing to put on a coat, he took it to the editor of the *Springfield Republican* and read it to him, too. The editor put it into a local news column. Within a day all of Springfield learned that Ted was going to Oxford.

There was one problem. Ted did not get the scholarship. Mr. Geisel nearly exploded when he heard the news at graduation. "But . . ." he sputtered. "But it was in the paper . . . All our friends . . . Everyone thinks . . ." He was quiet for a few moments. "How . . . ?" Ted held his breath. Would *Vater* erupt in rage, right there at the graduation ceremony?

"I didn't exactly say I *had* the scholarship,

Vater." Ted tried to protect himself.

Mr. Geisel raised his hand for silence. "I have decided," he finally said. "You will go to England. We will tell everyone you are in Oxford. That is a big enough city. There must be some school there you can get yourself into, with that clever tongue. And you will not come home until you learn something."

Ted, his luggage, and his typewriter sailed out of Boston on August 24, 1925. By October, he had talked his way into Lincoln College, the least expensive of Oxford's colleges. The only window in his room faced another stone wall and a small slice of lawn. Ted shivered. The room was as damp and as chilly as a dungeon. The dorms were five hundred years old. He wondered what they would be like in the winter.

It was grim in Oxford. Everywhere Ted looked, he saw the scars of the war. The Germans had caused it all. It made him feel shy somehow. The English students had a very different sense of humor. Here, his jokes just offended people. Ted began to keep to himself or speak just with other American students.

Ted fell hopelessly behind in his classes. He still enjoyed his writing, though. He thought he would write great novels. One night, he stayed up late in his room, typing. The next morning, a school official complained, "The clatter of your writing machine kept others awake."

Ted put the typewriter away. He sat in lectures and drew cartoons in his notebooks. The classes were full of studious Englishmen and equally serious young women. He began to feel alone.

"I have been watching you," a young woman said after class one day. Her accent was American and her smile was warm and bright. "I mean I've been watching you draw."

Ted blushed. He had drawn silly cows while a famous scholar talked on and on. "You're crazy to want to be a professor!" the girl told Ted. "What you really want to do is draw!" She glanced at his notebook. "You draw such wonderful flying cows." Ted looked down into her pale blue eyes. She was serious!

"I'm Ted Geisel," he said, extending his hand.

"I know," she said. "I'm Helen Marion Palmer." She brushed her soft brown hair back and looked up at the sound of a bell ringing from the chapel tower. "Oh, my goodness, I'm late for class!" she said. And she was gone.

Ted stumbled back up to his bedroom. This Helen was beautiful! She was an American. She was smart. He knew that because she worried about getting to classes on time. She did not think he had to spend his life as a professor. Best of all, she liked his silly drawings.

He could be an artist! A great weight lifted from his mind.

Ted and Helen spent day after day together, talking. Helen explained that she had been a teacher in Brooklyn for a few years before coming to Oxford. She was in her second year there, staying with her mother. Ted told her about the brewery and his night in jail. Helen's laughter made his heart soar. They began dating. Soon they split the cost and bought a motorcycle to tour England during school vacations. Oxford students were not supposed to have motorcycles. Ted tied dead ducks to the handlebars so it would look like they were hard at work making deliveries for a butcher shop.

The couple spent spring vacation motoring through Paris. The trip was a wild blur of new foods, new fashions, new kinds of buildings, and new scenery. Ted's mind spun with all these images. The feeling was delicious. Best of all, he had someone to share it with now—someone who loved his zany creative side.

Before they went back to school, Ted asked Helen to marry him. "Yes," she said.

As final exams neared, one of Ted's favorite professors pulled him aside. "You do not seem to be a serious Oxford student just yet. Take a year off and tour Europe. Visit museums. Draw. Read. Learn a little more history. Then perhaps you will be ready to study."

That sounded just right to Ted. He had learned more traveling for a few weeks than in all of his classes at Oxford. While Helen finished her degree, he traveled. When the Geisels came to visit, the family traveled all over Switzerland and Germany together. Later, Ted wandered from country to country with his American school chums from England. Helen took a teaching job in New York City and Ted finally went back home to Springfield. He never finished his degree at Oxford.

Now Ted sat at his drawing board upstairs, working harder than he ever had in his life. He wanted to marry Helen. In the 1920s, a man was expected to support his wife. Ted needed to make a living somehow. He sent countless cartoons, jokes, and funny essays to every magazine and newspaper he could think of. He sent copies to his Dartmouth friends, too, in case any of them knew an editor who might be interested. A year later, he sold his first cartoon to the *Saturday Evening Post*.

Part of him still dreamed of writing novels. That would make Red Smith proud. Mama and *Vater* would be thrilled. He decided to save his real name, Theodor Geisel, for serious writing. That first cartoon was signed only "Seuss." It showed a couple of clueless American tourists teetering on camels. They were comparing themselves to war heroes on a desert campaign. That one sale convinced Ted that his career had begun. He moved to

New York City within a month. A month later, he got a staff job as a weekly cartoonist for the humor magazine *Judge*. He had a desk at the office and earned seventy-five dollars a week.

Finally, he could marry Helen. With Whit Campbell as his best man, Ted and Helen exchanged vows at Helen's house on November 29, 1927. He was twenty-three. She was twenty-nine. They held a polite reception afterward. Then the real party began. Mr. Geisel took everyone to a secret club in New York City for champagne.

The young couple moved into an apartment in New York City. Ted kept submitting to other magazines. More and more work trickled in on top of his *Judge* assignments. He began making cartoons in series. One was called "Boids and Beasties." The first one showed a tower of turtles, one atop the other. To give it a silly sort of authority, he signed these cartoons "Dr. Theophrastus Seuss."

Most of his cartoons were political. They made fun of Prohibition. They laughed at crooked politicians. They mocked Hitler and the growing Nazi party. They were outrageous and smart-mouthed, as well as playful.

A twelve-year-old boy wrote for his autograph. It stunned Ted. It was the first time he realized that his work was not just making money for him. It was having a real effect on people. "If I can be an influence to one child in this great vice-ridden country," he told his friends, "my life has not been in vain." Ted put that letter next to Theophrastus on his drawing board and kept working.

In one of his *Judge* cartoons, Ted happened to draw a tube of bug spray. He decided to label it with the name of a real product called Flit. When the Flit company executives saw it there, they were thrilled. Standard Oil, the company that manufactured Flit, contacted Ted and asked if he would work for them, too, designing playful ads every few weeks during the buggy summer months. They offered more money than any of his Dartmouth classmates were making—even the ones who were successful lawyers. Ted began a new career in advertising.

His cartoon series "Quick, Henry, the Flit!" made everyone think of the bug spray with a smile. The work schedule left many months a year free for travel. He and Helen visited Europe, Egypt, Peru, and Greece.

In October of 1929, Ted lit his morning cigarette and read the headlines that announced a terrible fall in the prices at the New York Stock Exchange. All year, the radio by his drawing board reported worse and worse economic news. The whole country was enduring the Great Depression. In some cities, there were food riots. Ted passed endless lines of hungry, unemployed people waiting for food in New York streets. His own paychecks kept coming. Clever advertising was one of the few ways a company could stay in business, and Ted's talents were in demand.

He designed ads for many Standard Oil products. He made booklets. He even made a short movie. The company let his creativity run wild and paid him well. His cartoons appeared in magazines and as magazine covers, too. He illustrated a book of children's sayings that became a best-seller.

However, not everything was happy for him. Mrs. Geisel died six days before Ted's twenty-seventh birthday. His father was alone without his wife. His sister, Marnie, had married and had a baby, but her marriage had failed. She was alone with her baby. Helen had been ill, too. After an emergency surgery, they learned she could never have children. And all around the country, the economic news just kept getting worse.

In the summer of 1936, Ted and Helen could afford to take off on yet another deluxe ocean voyage to Europe. This was not a happy trip, though. The economy in Europe was as bad as at home. The rising power of Hitler's Nazi party had many of the people they met nervous. The whole continent seemed to be worried. What was Germany going to do? Ted was deeply upset.

"You can't do anything about this," Helen said, trying to take his mind off his fears. "You enjoyed writing the little books for Standard Oil. You loved illustrating that children's book. Perhaps you can write one yourself." Ted was not interested. The Geisels were glad to get aboard ship and come home.

The motor of this new ocean liner, the *Kungsholm,* had a different sound than older ships. Instead of a hum, the whole boat throbbed with a rhythm. To make things worse, an ocean storm kept Ted and Helen trapped below decks with the pulsing beat. Da-da-DA-da-da-DUM-DUM, the walls hummed. Da-DA-do-da-DUM. It was everywhere. In the floor, in the barroom, in the bed, and in Ted's brain. The endless rhythm was driving him crazy. He tried putting words to it. "'Twas the NIGHT before CHRIST-MAS, and ALL through the HOUSE" worked. For hours, he tried other words. He had nothing else to do while the storm raged on.

Shortly before they docked in New York, he came up with a rhyme. "And THAT is a story that no one can BEAT. And to THINK that I saw it on MULL-berry STREET," he said to Helen. She clapped her hands with excitement. In her eyes, Geisel saw the same joy and love that had greeted his wild sketches back in Oxford. That look had changed his life once. He had a feeling it was happening again.

And to Think!

At home, Ted sat down with a yellow lined pad and a pencil. He wrote a few words. He stared off into space. He erased the words he had written and tried again. He drank coffee. A story began to flow about Mulberry Street. Ted named it *A Story That No One Can Beat*. He smoked cigarettes and wrote, erased, and rewrote.

"Not quite," Helen would say when he read it to her. "It was better before." Or, "Almost . . ." She was a fussy editor, but Ted was even worse. Every word had to be perfect.

Every page had to be exciting. Every line had to lead the story, and the reader, on. And Ted wanted it all to be funny, too.

He did not laugh as he worked. He did not even smile. The jokes might be bubbling in his head, but they had to be said perfectly on the paper. He was still drawing Flit ads and cartoon series for Standard Oil. He met every deadline for his *Judge* magazine cartoons. They had taken a dark turn since his unsettling visit to Europe. But the gloom and worry did not show in his new book.

A Story That No One Can Beat was finally ready for illustrations. The main character was a creative little boy like Ted. The boy spins a tale of what he imagines in a parade on Mulberry Street in Springfield. The tale gets wilder and funnier as he talks. Ted carefully laid out drawings for each page. He used all the tricks he had learned from his advertising days to make the drawings and colors attractive. He had made people want to buy bug spray, motor oil, and magazines. Now he tried to make smaller people want to read his story. The illustrations matched the growing fantasy by getting bigger and sillier. The lines all led to the right to make a reader want to turn the page. The drawings and their painting took months.

He was still doing ads and cartoons, illustrating children's books by other people, and making huge fantasy animal head sculptures. Ted's mind was scattered over many projects, but *Story* had become very important to him.

Finally it was done. Ted, famous in so many ways, expected an easy sale when he sent it to a publisher. It was rejected. Repeatedly, Ted sent *A Story That No One Can Beat* to different publishers. The rejections just kept piling up. Ted got very discouraged. The project had taken far more work than he had expected. If no one bought it, all that time was wasted. Helen would not let him quit. "Where are you sending it next?" she would say firmly as each rejection arrived.

As a last resort, he decided to walk it right into a publisher's office downtown. If that didn't work, he would burn the whole project and forget about children's books.

The publisher had no interest in his *Story*. His fate decided at last, Ted walked home sadly.

"Say!" a voice behind him said. "Remember me? I'm Mike McClintoch. A year behind you at Dartmouth?" Ted did remember. The men chatted for a moment. Then Mike asked, "What's that under your arm?"

Ted looked down and shrugged. "My children's book," he said. "No one will publish it. I'm on my way home to burn it."

Mike looked astonished. "Ted," he said, "just three hours ago, I signed on to a new job. I am the children's book editor at Vanguard Press." The men looked at each other in stunned silence for a moment. "May

110

I look at what you have?" Ted nodded. When Mike glanced through the booklet Ted had carefully prepared, he said, "My office is across the street. Come upstairs with me. I want to show this to my boss."

The men huddled over Ted's work with James Henle, a Vanguard editor. "I like it," Henle said. "It's different. I like *different* books." This children's book was completely unlike others of the time. Instead of having a sweet, obedient hero, the little boy of Ted's book had a wild imagination that was not under his parents' control. He did not learn better manners or moral lessons. He just had fun exploring the freedom of his own mind.

James Henle stroked his chin. "I'm not too keen on the title, though."

Ted thought fast. "How about '*And To Think That I Saw It on Mulberry Street*'?"

James nodded. "It's different," he said. "Nice."

Ted renamed the main character "Marco,"

after James's son. Then the men signed a book contract. The book was not done, however. Ted fussed and fussed over printers' inks and cover paper, the wording of each line, and even the dedication to James's wife. He fretted over whether to call himself "Ted Geisel" or use the pseudonym Dr. Seuss. He chose Seuss, saving his Geisel name for a novel. *Mulberry Street* had to be perfect. He was still worrying over it when it went to press.

In September of 1937, fifteen thousand copies landed on bookstore shelves around the country. They sold for a dollar, a high price at the time. It was a big seller in Springfield, of course. The *New York Times* said it was "highly original and entertaining." Other reviews were good, too. The sales across the country were steady, but not outstanding. James Henle warned Ted that he would not get rich writing children's books.

"You need to write a few more books," he

told Ted. "That way youngsters and their parents will think of you as an author—not just as the Flit advertising man."

Ted went home. He paced around searching for an idea. When he looked in his closet, there were all his party hats: admirals' hats, firemen's helmets, nurses' caps, turbans, and ladies' go-to-church hats. He had been collecting them for years, using them for costumes and silly skits to make guests laugh. He went back to work at his tidy drawing board. The next book he brought to James Henle was *The 500 Hats of Bartholomew Cubbins.*

"But Ted," Henle said uneasily. "I think the King is just too mean. Shouldn't children's books have kind, fair adults?"

"Children know that sometimes they get in trouble even if they are doing everything right," Ted said. "And often it's people with lots of power, like my King Derwin, who aren't fair." He retold the story of President

Roosevelt's irritation with him. "Though it was the scoutmaster who'd miscounted the medals." He described how the government had made his family's business illegal, though they were running a successful, honest company. He also mentioned how his editorship at the Dartmouth humor magazine had been canceled overnight. He'd had no chance to argue.

"OK," James said. "But shouldn't this book end with a 'happily ever after'?"

"Didn't you get it?" Ted asked. "The little boy saves himself in the end by using the king's own selfishness."

"I like it," James Henle said. "But it surely is different. And, if you don't mind my asking, who is this 'Chrysanthemum-Pearl' in your dedication?"

Ted glanced out the window. He cleared his throat. "She is kind of a joke. We have no children," he said. "Never will." His voice was sad. "Our friends are always bragging about their perfectly wonderful little tots. That's when I spin completely outrageous stories about our own imaginary child, 'Chrysanthemum-Pearl.' That shuts them right up."

"Then she doesn't really exist?" Henle said. "Interesting."

The book came out in 1938. Once again, the reviews were nice and the sales were steady but not exciting.

Bennet Cerf bought a copy. He was an editor at Random House, a very large publishing company. He got a copy of *Mulberry Street*, too. Cerf liked to take chances on talented beginning authors in the hopes that their books would become best-sellers. He invited Ted out for a fancy lunch. "Big publishers like Random House have far more money for publicity, Ted," he said. "We can afford to print many more copies of a book. Often our authors earn much more." He let Ted think about that. "I like your style. Ted, I'd like to publish every single book you write," he said. "What are you working on now?"

"Maybe an adult book with lots of naked ladies," Ted teased. He was testing how serious Cerf was. He had actually been playing with that book idea. He knew Vanguard would never publish it.

"It's a deal," Cerf said. "I'll have a contract ready to sign by tomorrow morning."

Ted wrote and illustrated *The Seven Lady Godivas* for Random House. It was his only flop.

Then he went back to writing for children. For ideas, he remembered his own childhood. He thought about the stilts he had made. He remembered the Forest Park lion and Krazy Kat. He thought about breaking the teacher's rules in art class. These were just ideas. He needed a story.

The ideas grew for months. Since he had already done three books, he had a system. First, Ted thought a story through, and then he talked it out with Helen. Sometimes, he had to change it. Sometimes, he began all over again. Finally, he polished and reworked the wording. Helen helped edit it.

Then, Ted decided which words would go on each page to leave a reader eager to see what happens next. Helen made good suggestions. He sketched character after character and decided upon the best ones. He set up the illustrations on each page. They had to look zany but possible, so he bought a pair of stilts. He sketched them. He practiced walking on them, too. First, the illustrations were drawn faintly in pencil and then in ink. Finally, they were painted. Then, the fussing began to perfect the final book. Once it was delivered to the printer, Ted's work was done.

That spring, he visited Helen's old house. Her nieces were in the driveway, playing with stilts. "Excuse me," Ted said. He borrowed a pair and walked up the front stairs on them. Then he stilt-walked into the dining room.

He hobbled past all the fine china without breaking anything. "I learned how while doing research for my book," he explained to the startled girls.

In 1939, *The King's Stilts* went out to bookstores. In it, squads of patrol cats pace along the edge of the sea. The king tells Eric to break a law and do something very dangerous. In the end, the little boy has the courage to say no. His disobedience and common sense save a whole city.

Random House paid for a cross-country tour for Ted. They paid for food and lodging, train tickets, and taxi rides to bookstores and libraries. No matter how many interviews he gave or how many books he signed, the sales were disappointing.

Ted went back home to work on another book. His first idea started with a pale blue, troubled-looking elephant. Ted loved the image. The elephant had shown up in his cartoons of drunken men and African safaris.

Ted had drawn the woebegone beast in the parade down Mulberry Street, too. "I sketched him on thin tracing paper," he explained later, "and the breeze from an open window blew that sheet on top of a drawing I'd made of a tree." That story changed over the years, but the elephant in the tree, on a nest, on an egg grew in his mind.

"Osmer," he named the elephant at first. As he rewrote the story, it changed to "Bosco." In a much later draft, he became "Humphrey." A final draft fixed the elephant as "Horton." He borrowed that name from a Dartmouth classmate.

Ted had still not figured how to end the story. How did the elephant get down from the tree? Weeks and weeks passed. It was hard for Ted to concentrate on anything. He kept thinking about the frightening news from Europe. Ted listened closely, for the trouble was coming from Germany again.

A man named Adolph Hitler had whipped up

the patriotism of ordinary Germans. It changed into something very strange and very evil. He led them into thinking that only pureblooded Germans deserved to live in the country.

Hitler invented a political party for people who followed his beliefs. They were called the Nazis. These Nazis said the only true Germans were "Aryans." These people had pale white skin. Their eyes were light-colored and their hair was blond or light brown. Gypsies and Jews, homosexuals, Africans— *anyone* who looked or acted differently was bad for the country. Hitler seemed to be sending all non-Aryans away somewhere. There were terrible rumors about what happened to these people, but no proof. Hitler seemed capable of anything. When he sent armies to take over other countries for the Aryan race, Ted's blood ran cold.

Ted had been to Germany. He had seen Hitler's troops, nearly all blond and well armed. He had seen the fear in the eyes of other Europeans. He knew how deeply passions ran in the Homeland. He was afraid of what was happening—and he could not understand why other Americans did not see the danger.

Then the Nazi army marched into France. Hitler's men invaded Paris, bombing and killing, looting and destroying as they went. Rumors flew about what else they might be doing to their own citizens, the ones who were not part of Hitler's "Master Race."

"We have to stop the Nazi sickness while there is still time!" some people argued. Most people, still struggling from the economic depression, said, "We have enough troubles of our own right here." "I like being isolated and safe." "That isn't our problem." "Let them fight their own battles."

Ted went after these isolationists in his cartoons. He drew them as ostriches hiding their heads in the sand, ignoring the danger, while their great fat bodies were unguarded.

He wrote wickedly funny essays and touching news stories, too. Ted used all of his talents to try to get people to help their European friends before it was too late. The United States had signed treaties with them, after all, right after the last war ended.

That thought helped power the elephant book. Horton makes a promise and keeps it, 100 percent. Even when all of his friends make fun of him, he is loyal. That is what Ted was fighting for: acting to protect the defenseless. He was so upset by the news of the day, that it was Helen who finally solved the problem of how the book would end. She suggested what would come out of a fierce loyalty—a new kind of bond entirely. Finally, the egg that the elephant has been baby-sitting for so long hatches. "MY WORD! It's something brand new! IT'S AN ELEPHANT-BIRD!!"

Cerf was delighted with the book. He sent Ted a payment early, to help the Geisels buy a little house on the California shore. Traveling around the world had become too dangerous. The Geisels did not want to live in New York any more. Ted did not want to go back to Springfield where his family was, either. Ted needed a new place, quiet enough to let him work in peace. His cartoons, writings, and illustrations could be delivered to New York by mail. He promised to fly to New York to deliver his books to Cerf whenever they were ready.

Horton Hatches the Egg was an immediate success. It outsold his other four books combined within weeks. It was funny. It was rich with meaning. It was the first Seuss book with a clear moral. It made children and parents feel good.

But Ted knew there were problems in the world that were bigger than children could solve. Another war seemed likely now. Ted decided to give up writing children's books. He thought he had more important work to do.

Major Geisel

Ted watched world peace crumbling around him. He felt he could not just keep writing children's books. After all, it was the adults who were making such a mess of things. Ted focused on political cartooning. Perhaps, he thought, he could change some minds about the way things were going.

A new newspaper had just started in New York City. It was called *PM* and was known for its liberal viewpoint. A friend handed a cartoon of Ted's to the editor. *PM* printed it within days. At first he did three, and later, five political cartoons for *PM* every week.

One series of his cartoons showed Adolf Hitler as a spoiled little baby in diapers. Baby Adolf demanded his own way in Europe. Many people in the United States still did not think he and his Fascist ally in Italy, Benito Mussolini, were real threats to world peace. Ted knew differently. *Newsweek* said his cartoons were stirring up "hornets' nests" of reaction. He had people everywhere thinking, talking, and acting.

Ted was thirty-eight when Japan bombed Hawaii, on December 7, 1941. The surprise attack stunned Ted as it did everyone else. The United States declared war on Japan. Days later, Congress declared war on Germany and Italy, too. This was the Second World War in Ted's life. The first time he was too young to fight. Now, Ted was too old to be a foot soldier, doing battle in the streets. That did not mean he sat home. He fought in his own way.

The United States government assigned several posters to him. "Starve the squander bug," one said. It told Americans to conserve resources at home so there would be plenty to send to our troops. Ted's silly design also made people laugh. They felt good about the service they were doing.

Ted did not think he was doing enough. He joined a special creative unit of the army. They knew what gifts Captain Theodor Seuss Geisel brought to the military. After basic training, he was assigned to work in a Hollywood studio. Instead of firing bullets, he would be firing off information to the troops that make them laugh—and would make them care.

The army rented a Fox movie studio near Sunset Boulevard. A famous movie director, Frank Capra, was in charge of this "Signal Corps." The soldiers wore army uniforms, practiced marching and shooting, and ate food prepared by army cooks. There were no regular army barracks to live in, though. Ted and Helen rented a house nearby, and he drove to work every day.

Soldiers do not earn much money. The Geisels had to sell their New York City apartment. Helen went to work, too. She wrote and sold three children's books. They did not rhyme and she did not illustrate them, but they made money for the family. Helen was too worried to be happy in her new work or her new home.

California's huge coastline faces Japan. People there watched for submarine attacks. They feared attacks by air, too, like the one in Hawaii. Ted had to keep the windows of his house covered with dark shades. That way no light would show at night and make the house a target in a sneak attack. The government feared Japanese spies in this country, too. Ted remembered what it had been like as a German American during World War I. People had stopped trusting him. Now people feared Japanese Americans. Thousands of innocent people were put into American prison camps in case they were spies. To keep Helen feeling safe during this scary time, Ted got her a big dog. The playful Irish setter did more than protect—it made her laugh.

At work, Ted was searching for laughter, too. Military writing is usually dull. The Capra team wanted to change that. They made a series of cartoon films. They starred a young army soldier called "Private Snafu" who could never do anything right. "SNAFU" was a term soldiers use to mean "Situation Normal—All Fouled Up." Soldiers on bases everywhere roared with laughter at Private Snafu's disasters. They also learned what *not* to do about their health, security, army discipline, and mental focus.

Ted wrote the scripts of these training films. Frank Capra took one look at an early draft and sighed. "The first thing you have to do," he said, picking up a blue pencil, "is find out if you're saying anything." He underlined only those sentences that were really important to the plot. "You can throw out all those other words," Frank said. It was a lesson Ted never forgot. He enjoyed writing and animating films. His movies were so funny and so clever he won an Oscar. Because it was wartime, though, the ceremony was quiet.

In a little over a year, American troops began to move into Europe. Frank Capra thought Ted was ready to do his own film. *Your Job in Germany* was supposed to show soldiers how to occupy and rebuild areas the Nazis had lost. To do research for it, Ted went to Europe while there was still fighting in Germany. He was now Major Ted Geisel.

It was a staggering trip. Ted had traveled throughout the area before the war and loved it. Now, everything was different. France, Belgium, the Netherlands—it was all changed. Priceless old buildings were bombed to ruins. Bridges lay toppled into rivers. Forests were dead, shredded by gunfire. The people were hungry and hollow-eyed with fear and exhaustion.

Army friends managed to sneak him into newly freed areas of Germany. Things were even worse there. In Germany, Ted had relatives, and memories of old family stories. The Nazis had ruined everything. Talking with German teenagers left Ted horrified. They had been taught for years by Nazis in Nazi schools. Even their picture books were full of twisted Nazi ideas. These children took all the prejudices they had been taught as true.

They really believed that the blue-eyed, blond-haired, Aryan Germans were the super race. They thought Aryans had every right to take over the world because everyone else was flawed. They believed that non-Aryans were useful only as servants or slaves. It was chilling to hear these young people and their little brothers and sisters. Everyone thought the same.

Ted looked at the children sadly. Now they would hear the truth, at last, but they had a lot of lies to unlearn.

While Ted was in Europe, the Americans dropped atomic bombs on a city in Japan called Hiroshima. When it was safe, the Army allowed Major Ted Geisel to go to the bomb site. He saw the nightmare of destruction from just one atomic explosion. The huge city was now rubble. Its men, women, and children were dead or poisoned with radiation. Another city, Nagasaki, had been bombed, too. Faced with the nuclear might of America, Japan surrendered. The Second World War was over.

Ted still had months left to serve in the army. He flew home to California and began working on a film about the Japanese. It tried to break down people's prejudices about their recent enemies. The United States government thought he had gone too far in making the Japanese seem like regular people who had been raised with all the wrong ideas. The Army would not allow *Know Your Enemy—Japan* to be shown.

When Ted left the army, he was well-known among moviemakers. A film company asked him to work on a film that would show people how to avoid a third world war. Together, they reworked Ted's rejected film about Japan. It came out in 1947 as *Design for Death*, and was nominated for an Academy Award. The ceremony was lavish and the Geisels dressed up for their red carpet stroll. As his film was announced as Best Documentary, Ted walked onto the stage. He accepted the Oscar statue, and listened to the applause.

Ted's movie had won, but he did not enjoy making it. He felt that there were just too many people making decisions on a film. Most of his creative ideas were challenged and changed by others. "I'd rather make my

own mistakes than have squads of people make them," he told friends.

Ted longed for the creative control he had when he wrote and illustrated picture books. Millions of soldiers were flooding back home now. They were starting new families. They would all need books for their children.

Once Ted had thought that adult books, magazines, and cartoons were the way to change the world. But in Germany, he had seen how powerful the Nazis had become by twisting young minds. Ted knew he could reach many, many thousands of children through books. There were things he thought American youngsters should know. He knew they learned best through laughter and brightly colored, funny pictures. Besides, he loved working on picture books.

It had been seven years since *Horton Hatches the Egg* had been so successful. Ted picked up the phone and dialed his old editor, Bennet Cerf.

Johnny Can't Read?

"I'll go back to writing and illustrating books for children," Ted told Bennet Cerf. "But I want to stay here in California where I can walk around in my pajamas all day long." The Random House editor agreed to work with Ted through the mail and by phone, with a visit when a book was due. Instead of moving back to New York, Ted and Helen bought a classic old house in Los Angeles. Ted painted zany murals on the walls. He put his big playful sculptures in every room. It looked like a fun house now, but Ted worked very hard there.

For ideas, he went back to his childhood again, as he had with *And To Think That I Saw It on Mulberry Street.* This time he remembered fishing trips in Springfield's Forest Park with his father. He thought about stopping by Deesels' fish market on the way home to buy fish. Ted paced and sketched, wrote, and threw page after page away. Slowly the rhymes and story for *McElligot's Pool* came together.

Ted slaved over the illustrations. He did not want them to look like a comic book. He wanted them to be different from his advertising work, too. He needed his own "look." When he found it, he demanded that the publisher reproduce the beautiful watercolor washes exactly. Finally, he dedicated the book to his father, "the World's Greatest Authority on Blackfish, Fiddler Crabs, and Deesel Trout."

All the work paid off. The American Library Association named *McElligot's Pool* a

Caldecott Honor book. The prize and a prestigious silver sticker went to one of the best-illustrated books of the entire year. The book sold well through book clubs, too. It was a tremendous success.

During the war, Helen had written three children's books on her own. They did not make her famous like her husband. Now, Helen listened to Ted's stories, advising him through every book. She also handled every household chore, from floor-sweeping to bill-paying. This was how almost all families divided the work in the years after the war: The man earned the money and the woman took care of the home.

Ted remembered the war as he searched for ideas for his next book. One rainy night in Belgium, he had heard a thoroughly soaked soldier grumble, "Rain, always rain. Why can't we have something different for a change?" Ted imagined something different—and named it "oobleck." He pictured it falling on his old character, Bartholomew. His publisher had said that watercolors like those in *McElligot's Pool* were too expensive to print in every book. "Fine," Ted said, and designed this book to be in all black and white. Only the gooey green of the oobleck required colored inks.

When it came out, *Bartholomew and the Oobleck* won another Caldecott Honor for Ted's clever illustrations. Ted was already working on a new Horton book and a book called *If I Ran the Zoo*. His energy was enormous. Ted was drawing ads again, too, and writing stories for Capitol Records. Capitol bought *Gerald McBoing-Boing* and made a record of it. Later, an animated feature was created of the story. That film won Ted another Oscar. Four more *Gerald McBoing-Boing* movies followed and then CBS television produced thirteen episodes of the *Gerald McBoing-Boing Show.*

Meanwhile, the producers talked Ted into

a new project. They wanted him to write a story for another movie with live actors. Ted told himself it could not be as bad as working on the Japan film. He was wrong.

He started his new story idea with memories of his sister Marnie's endless piano practices. That was too dull for a movie, so he exaggerated to make it funnier. He wrote a movie script about an insane piano teacher named Dr. T, who commands a whole army of boys to practice. He has a giant piano where he forces them to play for days.

The 5,000 Fingers of Dr. T was difficult to film from the first. There was the normal wrestling over the writing and wording. There were also crowds of child actors to manage. The director paid them well for their work, but he made a mistake. He gave the money to the boys instead leaving it with their parents. When the filming paused one day, the young cast decided to get hot dogs. They rushed down to the company cafeteria and gobbled as many hot dogs as they could buy. After the break, they came back onto the set. They took their places at a vast, fake piano. Suddenly one boy threw up. The sight and smell made the next boy hurl, too. "This started a chain reaction," Ted told a friend later, "causing one after another of the boys to go queasy in the greatest mass upchuck in the history of Hollywood."

That scene was cut, the set was cleaned up, and the film was completed. It was not a success in theaters. Ted was angry with himself for ever going back into films. He knew what he enjoyed—writing and illustrating books.

Ted got a little bit of money for every one of his books that sold. Ten percent of the price was always set aside as a royalty for the author/illustrator. The rest of the money that people paid for the book went to buy the paper and ink and pay the printing costs. It also covered the advertising, the editor's and publisher's salaries, and some of the bookstore and publishing company's expenses. Ted's books were very popular and he wrote a new one every year. All those little royalty payments began to add up. In addition, Helen had money left to her when her parents died.

Ted decided that he was earning enough money to quit all his other jobs. Now he would focus on what he loved most. The Geisels decided to buy another house where Ted could work without interruption. They chose a strange tower high atop a mountain in La Jolla, California. From its broad upper windows, Ted could look out over the Pacific Ocean. That, he decided, would be a perfect office. The Geisels had to add bedrooms, a living room, and a kitchen to the bottom of the tower before they could move in.

Once in their new home, the Geisels were busy in La Jolla. Ted's books kept coming. He often used them to counter the prejudices he had faced in his youth and the wrongs he had seen in the world. For instance, the

Sneeches, in *The Sneeches and Other Stories*, hate each other for no good reason except that some of them have stars on their bellies and some don't. Ted hoped that children would learn from the story that skin color and surface differences don't really matter. In *Horton Hears a Who,* a tiny little creature saves the day. That was Ted's way of saying that a young person is just as important as any adult. In *On Beyond Zebra,* he invited children to think beyond the letters of the alphabet—and everything else—that teachers teach them. Ted knew this was an important message. He had seen what had happened in Nazi schools where nobody had told the students that they could think for themselves. Ted repeated the message a different way in *Oh, the Thinks You Can Think.*

Year after year the books came, written and illustrated by Ted, edited by Helen. They were busy in their community, too. Helen entertained several times a week, throwing fancy dinner parties. Ted led a fight against the billboards that had begun to crowd the beautiful California freeways. The Geisels traveled, internationally and within the country. In 1953, Ted agreed to speak at a Dartmouth graduation ceremony. The college was going to give him another degree for all the good he had done for soldiers and for children. With this honorary doctorate, Ted would actually be *Doctor* Seuss at last.

Although she had been feeling tired, Helen planned three birthday dinners the week that Ted turned fifty. On March 2, 1954, a dinner guest asked, "Did you see your name this week in *Life* magazine? That's a nice birthday gift!" He explained that a famous writer, John Hershey, had learned some bad news about American children. Many of them were not learning to read in school. They were growing into illiterate adults. Hershey thought it had to do with their schoolbooks. The stories kids were given to read were all about sweet, obedient, little white children whose clothes were always clean and whose faces were always smiling.

"Nobody cares about goody-goody characters like that!" Helen said.

"That's why Hershey mentioned 'Dr. Seuss,'" the guest said. "He wished that all kids' books were as much fun as Ted's."

After the guests had gone home, Ted followed Helen into the kitchen. He watched in horror as she crumpled to the floor in pain. Helen's feet and legs were too sore to support her. She went to bed, and two days later finally allowed Ted to take her to a clinic. She staggered inside. By the next morning, the pain and a strange numbness had spread through Helen's body. Paralysis followed. Helen could not move her leg or arm muscles. She couldn't swallow, either. She was terrified. So was Ted. The doctors put her on life support to keep her breathing.

Helen hovered near death for weeks. The trip to Dartmouth, like everything else, was put on hold. Finally, Helen began swallowing on her own. The long, long road to recovery began. Helen needed help relearning how to do everything: talk, walk, dial a phone, button her own clothes. Ted did everything he could to help, but her progress was slow and discouraging.

The first copy of his newest book arrived and cheered both Geisels. They needed every bit of Ted's good humor during the months of Helen's physical therapy. She had always nagged Ted to give up smoking. Now, to make her feel better, he promised to quit. He threw away his cigarettes and planted strawberry seeds in his old corncob pipe. It made Helen laugh. Ted kept smoking in private so it would not upset her. A year after he had first been invited, Ted finally went to Dartmouth and got his doctorate.

Soon after that, an old friend, William

Spaulding, invited Ted to come to Boston. Spaulding was the head of the Houghton-Mifflin publishing company's education branch. Over dinner, he and Ted talked about a new book called *Why Johnny Can't Read*, by Rudolf Flesch. It showed just how badly American students were doing. Flesch thought that television and comic books were making pictures more important than words. Spaulding wondered if he and Ted could do something about the problem.

"Write me a story that first graders can't put down," he dared Ted. "Here's a list of the 225 first words a beginning reader learns. Make a great story up from this list and I will publish it. I'll make sure it gets into schools." Ted loved the challenge. If the first book children read made them laugh aloud, they would want to read more. The more they read, the easier reading would become. These children would want to read more books. Ted felt he could make a real difference in literacy that way.

There was a problem, however. He had agreed to let Bennet Cerf at Random House publish all of his books. Ted called Cerf and pleaded for the chance to write beginner books for schools. "That's fine," Cerf finally said. "But Random House gets to sell them in stores." Ted went home with a new cause and a list of simple words.

"There are no adjectives!" he wailed to Helen. Her legs and feet ached all the time and she was always exhausted. The doctors told her it was Guillian-Barré Syndrome that had affected her nerves so badly. She might feel fine again someday, they said, but she should feel lucky to be alive at all. Helen pretended to be healing and used her energy to encourage Ted.

He paced his office. He drank gallons of coffee and smoked cartons of cigarettes, staring at the list of dull words. He wanted the book to rhyme, since poems are fun to hear again and again. Little children need to repeat things to learn them well. Ted lay on the orange couch in his office mindlessly tossing his old toy dog, Theophrastus, up into the air and catching it. Ted almost gave up on the whole project. One day he decided to use the first two rhyming words on the list as part of his title. "Cat," he read, and then, "Hat."

Ted had loved cats since drawing the lion at the Forest Park Zoo. Cats had appeared in many of his cartoons and books. Now he began drawing them again. He played with hats and neckties, rubbery legs and silly faces. It was many more months before he had a story, and months more before he got the words and the beat to work perfectly. Next came the pictures, lively and full of naughty fun. Ted used nothing but the most intense blue and red to make the illustrations. That made them vibrate with energy. Bennet Cerf was thrilled. So was Spaulding. They published *The Cat in the Hat* in 1957.

This was a book like no other. The children

in the story were home alone. They let a weird stranger in who made a mess of their house. The strange Cat was not sorry, though he did clean up. The children were left deciding whether to tell their mother the truth or not. The end of the book was not tidy. Did it all really happen or did the children imagine it? Should they tell the truth? Ted ended the book with the question: What would you do…?

The book was a wild success with kids, teachers, parents, and critics. Sales were so good that Bennet Cerf's wife, Phyllis, asked Ted to do a whole series of books. She would publish them. Ted would be her partner in this new company. All of their books would be for first-grade readers. This "Beginner Books" series would have the Cat in the Hat logo on the cover. Ted's regular books were about the size of notebook paper. The Beginner Books would be made smaller to fit a young reader's little hands. But they would be packed with just as much fun and wordplay.

Ted had to think about it. "Could I keep doing my other books?" he asked. "Can I decide what books go into the series? Can Helen be in this company, too? The excitement would be good for her." Phyllis Cerf agreed to everything.

Ted was still finishing one of his "big books." He had promised a Christmas book to Bennet Cerf years earlier and it was finally ready. He started working on a Beginner Book with Helen, too. Ted thrived when he was overworked. Helen was different. She had less energy since she'd been sick. Ted promised to go on a vacation with her as soon as *How the Grinch Stole Christmas* came out.

The Grinch was Ted's second huge success in 1957.

There were more successes as other authors began to write for the new Beginner Books line. Ted produced *The Cat in the Hat*

Comes Back and many others. He didn't always have the time now to illustrate all of the books he wrote. When others drew the pictures, Ted did not want to sign the books "Dr. Seuss." He was still saving the name "Theodor Geisel" in case he wrote a grand novel someday. Now he used his father's old pseudonym, "Theo. LeSeig."

The Beginner Books company was making a great deal of money. In the year ending in August 1960, it had sold far more than a million dollars' worth. It was also causing stress between Phyllis Cerf and the Geisels. They could not agree on new authors and which books to publish. Stress seemed to make Helen's disease worse. It also distracted Ted from writing. Bennet Cerf came up with an answer. Random House would buy and run the whole series. Phyllis would not be part of it any more. Helen was relieved. Ted's mind was off and working on a new challenge.

"I'll bet you fifty dollars that you can't write

a Beginner Book with just fifty words," Cerf said. Ted took the bet, but it took months of work. Often, Ted decided it was impossible. Then, he would give it another try. Finally, Ted won the bet with *Green Eggs and Ham.*

The next few years, Ted worked on Beginner Books, like *Fox in Socks* and *Hop on Pop.* Stan and Jan Berenstain began to write about bears for the series and handle some of the editorial work. Helen and Ted kept up a wild schedule of travel and parties, though it seemed that Helen's health was failing again.

Audrey and Grey Dimond became regular visitors at Helen's parties. Grey was a doctor at the clinic where Helen had first gone with her strange nerve disease. Audrey was a lively, warm young woman with a sense of humor almost as playful as Ted's. She had been a nurse, so she was warm and caring with Helen. The two couples vacationed together. They often shared dinners.

They met to celebrate a successful TV special made from *The Grinch* in 1966. Later that month, Ted and Helen took a vacation on a boat with other friends. Ted was as energetic as always. He figured he had twenty good years ahead of him—years when he could write books and party with his friends. Helen seemed sad and withdrawn. She just wanted to go home. Since her illness, it had taken every bit of her energy to keep up a cheery, carefree front. Now she seemed too tired to manage.

When she got back to the tower house, everyone thought Helen would be fine.

They were wrong. Helen knew she was getting weaker. The disease was going to kill her. She decided that the effort to look well all the time was not worth it. One morning, Helen got up before Ted and went down to the kitchen. She took enough sleeping pills to stop her breath, her heartbeat, and her painful struggles forever.

Fighting for the Future

Helen's death stunned her friends. Nobody knew she was depressed enough about her disease to kill herself. A note she left was full of love for Ted, but he was devastated. He had not just lost his best friend. For forty years, Helen had been his creative partner, too. She edited his words, gave him ideas, and handled all his business matters. He felt lost and terribly alone.

He wandered around his empty house for weeks before he could make any decisions about his life. Slowly he began working again, losing himself in the playful rhythms and bright colors of his first "Bright and Early Book," *The Foot Book*. It was for even younger children than his Beginner Books. Ted redecorated his office. Over the next months, he spent time with cheerful old friends.

He had never known how truly unhappy Helen was with her life. His friend Audrey Dimond had also kept a secret from him. Her marriage was breaking up. Her life was adrift, too. She wanted to leave her husband, Grey. She was eighteen years younger than Ted, but her energy level and her humor matched his. So did her loneliness.

Ted and Audrey were married on August 5, 1978, nearly a year after Helen's death. Ted's new stepdaughters, Lark and Lea, were teenagers. Though the house in La Jolla was enlarged to make rooms for Audrey's daughters, the girls spent most of their time in New York with their father.

Ted's next book, *I Can Lick 30 Tigers Today! And Other Stories*, was dedicated to Audrey. Together, the new Geisel couple made a fine creative partnership. Audrey liked to travel as much as Ted did. In the first year of their marriage, they took a trip around the world, through Japan, India, and Turkey, ending up in his beloved Paris.

Traveling always gave Ted inspiration. Although he went right back to work on his Beginner and Bright and Early Books, a big new idea was brewing. The area near his home was being built up. New houses, stores, offices, and condominiums sprouted everywhere. There were no forests left, no broad fields full of wildflowers and butterflies. He had seen the same thing around the world. People were crowding out nature.

Ted had helped fight against billboards in his own community. Now that his books were printed in many different languages, the whole world was his community. He had made a huge difference in what kind of books children saw in schools everywhere. His stories made the points he cared about. Children, no matter how small, deserved respect. People in authority were not always right. Anyone can make a difference. Young people learned these messages as they laughed and learned how to read.

Perhaps it was time, Ted thought, to teach a lesson to the world about saving the environment. He made dozens of starts. He filled his wastebasket over and over with ideas that did not work. He made every deadline for the "little books." He just could not get anywhere with the characters and a lighthearted story about a more serious subject.

Ted and Audrey traveled to Africa, touring the still-wild countryside and the crowded cities. When he came home, he was ready to write *The Lorax*. In this story, an old character called the Once-ler tells a young stranger how beautiful his town once was. Ted's drawings showed the blue skies and fluffy Truffula tree

159

forest, and the colorful birds, animals, and sparkling water that had once been there. The Once-ler had ordered every Truffula tree to be cut down to fuel his factories. There was nothing left now except one last Truffula seed. The Once-ler gives it to the stranger with a warning that "unless someone like you cares a whole awful lot," things will never get better.

This book had a stronger moral and deeper colors than Dr. Seuss's readers expected. It wasn't funny. *The Lorax* was published in 1971, just as the environmental movement was getting started in America. People were not ready for it.

The giant Sequoias in northern California were being cut down by timber companies. *The Lorax* made several loggers' children angry with their fathers. Some families in one logging town told their local library to get rid of the book. They did not want their children to think that cutting forests down to the ground was bad.

160

Having people try to ban his book did not upset Ted. It told him he was doing a good thing. He remembered the German children who had gone to Nazi schools where everyone had to think one way. Those children had grown up thinking that they were completely right and everyone else in the world was wrong. They had never been allowed to think for themselves. *The Lorax* made people, young and old, think.

The book was translated into many languages and made into a TV special the next year. When people complained that it had a moral, Ted said, "It's impossible to tell a story without a moral—either the good guys win, or the bad guys win."

In a way, Ted was winning. His *Lorax* influenced millions of first- and second-graders. Ten years later, they were ready to join the environmental movement. *The Lorax* became his favorite book.

Now in his seventies, Ted was aging. So

were his friends. Bennet Cerf, his longtime editor, died. Ted had to learn to work with other editors. This was not easy. He quarreled with the staff of the Beginner Books company and finally quit as its president. He slowed down in his writing. His illustrations were changing, too.

Ted could not see well. He had cataracts, a clouding in the lenses of his eyes. He also had glaucoma, which can slowly cause blindness. Ted had several operations and many treatments to try to save his eyesight. The change in his vision showed up in his drawings. The lines, once smooth and sure, became sketchy. The colors were strange too—murkier and grayer.

Ted kept writing and traveling. Audrey saw that he was happier when he did not have to sit and squint at his drawing board. She encouraged him to give more speeches. She arranged more book signings around the world. She also coaxed him into growing a beard. She could not keep him from smoking, though, no matter how she nagged.

Ted was fabulously famous. The post office in La Jolla began dreading the day of March 2. Every year more than twenty thousand birthday cards flooded the mail, all addressed to Dr. Seuss.

Eye surgery after his seventy-fifth birthday finally fixed Ted's color vision. He had the aches and pains of an elderly man, but his energy did not stop. He kept writing and illustrating Beginner Books, partying and playing tricks on friends. In 1981, though, Ted had a heart attack. He almost died.

Quit smoking. When he heard it this time, Ted had to listen. "All that nicotine in your circulatory system almost killed you. It will, soon, unless you stop smoking." This was not his wife nagging. It was Ted's doctor.

Ted quit for good this time. He did it playfully, as he did everything. Ted got out his old corncob pipe again. This time he filled it with

peat moss and planted it with radish seeds. It gave him the familiar feeling of something in his mouth while he worked. When he had the impulse to light up, he grabbed an eyedropper full of water and squirted it onto the seeds. It made people laugh, and that made Ted feel good.

Pipe and cigarette smoking had done more than just damage his heart. At his next dentist appointment, Ted learned he had cancer in his mouth. "Smokers often get this," the dentist told him. "It will kill you if you don't treat it."

Ted let the doctors put a radioactive bead into the flesh under his tongue. For five days, the radiation poisoned the dangerous cancer cells. Ted stayed in the hospital for two more weeks, frail and sick.

"We think we got all the cancer," the doctors told him. "But we can't be sure."

Ted headed for his drawing board as soon as he could. He had another big idea. He saw a problem happening in the world that he thought he might help solve. That kind of inspiration had made *The Lorax* an important book. Ted was ready to do it again. This time, he wanted to stop the Cold War.

He had lived through two "hot" World Wars of terrible violence. This battle was different. It was being fought with threats. Both Russia and the United States had nuclear bombs. Both countries kept their bombs aimed at each other. Whenever the United States made more bombs, Russia did, too. The money that they were spending was needed for schools and parks, food and roads. Instead, it was spent on weapons. Ted had seen how just one atomic bomb had leveled an entire city in Japan. There were enough bombs sitting ready during the Cold War to kill everyone on earth ten times over—and still more were being made.

Sooner or later, one might go off by mistake. Then World War Three would start.

Ted was afraid. So were many other people.

He paced in his office. How could he stop it? Ted could start the change with a children's book, but he had to have a story. It had to rhyme. It had to make people laugh. He stared out his window at the Pacific Ocean. He lay on his couch and tossed Theophrastus. He sketched away for weeks.

At last he had it. Within a year, *The Butter Battle Book* was ready to go to press. In the story, two cultures threaten to destroy each other for something as silly as buttered bread. It was absurd. It was scary, too. There was no happy ending. When it was read at the publisher's office, the sales staff stood up and applauded. "Is this for children or adults?" they asked. In the end, it didn't matter.

Suddenly, though, Ted was too busy to care. The doctors found that the last bits of his mouth cancer had spread into his neck. In an operation, the new tumor was taken out.

Ted's recovery was painful and slow. It took three months before he was ready to get back to work, and he had to wear a high collar to hide the terrible scar.

The Butter Battle Book was published on Ted's eightieth birthday, in 1984.

The book made it onto the *New York Times* best-seller list. It was translated into many languages and sold worldwide. Once again, some parents tried to ban the book. It was even made into a television special in Russia. This was just what Ted had hoped would happen. People around the world were talking about the foolishness of the Cold War and how to end it.

The greatest American honor any writer can hope for is a Pulitzer Prize. It is only given to writers of adult books—but now Ted got the award. The surprise award meant that Ted was on the front page of newspapers, on television shows, speaking at major conferences and universities, and meeting President Reagan at the White House.

This was the president who had ordered all the bombs for the United States. As it turned out, Russia lost the Cold War. It was not because they had fewer bombs. It was because they ran out of money for the basics before the United States did. With Russia out of business, the arms race was over. Reagan shook Ted's hand. Ted's mouth hurt, but he could not stop his smile. Around the world, children were reading *The Butter Battle Book*. They would grow up remembering its message: Never get so excited about war-making that you forget there are other ways to solve problems.

Theophrastus

For many years, Ted's life had become a series of doctor's appointments and treatments. Experts fought to keep his cancer under control. He sat in waiting rooms, sketching. He waited on stretchers, sketching. He made silly pictures of his doctors, of the nurses, and of their high-tech equipment. Ted's mouth hurt terribly. He was tired most of the time, and cranky—he was not making books and he missed it.

Audrey encouraged him to go out. When he had the energy, he had dinner with friends.

Now and then, he spoke to groups. The scars in his mouth made his voice slurred. It made him shy. At Princeton University in New Jersey, he was given yet another honorary college degree. When he stood in front of all the students, he did not have to talk. They all jumped to their feet at once. Together they yelled every word of his book, *Green Eggs and Ham.*

It was thrilling for Ted to hear the words he had rhymed so many years earlier. He had touched those young adults when they were little. They still remembered it today. Ted felt a new surge of energy. When he got home, he looked at the doctor's office sketches he had been making. They could be another book!

It took longer than usual for eighty-year-old Ted to come up with a story and rhymes that would make people smile. The tests and treatments he had to go through were scary and painful. It took a lot of energy just to keep going. That became the story of the book. That and the price of all the treatments.

Ted could afford anything, of course. His books had sold by the millions in many, many countries. From each one he had gotten a royalty. He had used some of the money to buy up as much open land as he could get around his hilltop home. He gave a lot of money away to libraries and universities, to children's charities, and to museums. Still, he was vastly wealthy. His money did not change his personality. He still cracked jokes with the doctors and winked at the nurses.

You're Only Old Once, a Book for Obsolete Children came out on Ted's eighty-second birthday. It was another wild success. People bought it for their little children. They got it for their elderly grandparents, too. It made everyone feel better about all the scary treatments they might get.

It was clear that all the medical treatments in the world could not keep Ted's old body going much longer. A friend asked if Ted would allow a show of his life's artwork in a museum in nearby San Diego. Ted helped to choose the pieces and write the booklet that went along with the show. It included very early artwork, ads, book illustrations, sculptures, and the paintings that Ted had done just for himself.

It was a marvelous show. It moved across the country from museum to museum. Ted and Audrey came along when they could. They spent time in Springfield, Massachusetts, too, where his story had begun. Everywhere, crowds of people waited to see Ted and to get his autograph. At the end, he went home, happy but very, very tired.

He was in pain, too. His mouth hurt and his jawbone was infected. His hearing was failing and gout made it hard for him to walk. Still, he wrote another Beginner Book. He did not illustrate it, though.

Now, Ted made a change in one of his oldest books. He had grown and changed throughout his life. Starting with the differences he had made in the *Jack-O-Lantern* at Dartmouth, he had fought against his own prejudices. When he looked at *And To Think That I Saw it on Mulberry Street* now, he knew the yellow-faced "Chinaman" he had put in the book was just a crude joke. He painted the scene again, changing the color of the man's skin and the shape of his eyes. He also changed his wording from a "Chinaman" to a "Chinese man." And Ted insisted that all the *Mulberry Street* books that would ever be printed again would have these changes. Ted truly felt now that everyone deserved respect.

He had said it in books and proved it in his life. Now he had a few more things to say. He rounded up odd sketches he had and pinned them to the cork walls of his study. He rearranged them, sat down, and studied the effect. He rested some. Then he wrote rhymes. This was going to be his last book, and he knew it. There were things he had learned and wanted to pass on to his fans and to children everywhere.

The cancer was back and it was much worse. Ted did not want any more treatments. Random House did not think there was any chance he would finish another book. They were willing to do anything for him. When he asked, an editor flew from New York to La Jolla to help with the book. From ten A.M. to six P.M., the office hours he'd kept all his life, he fussed over colors, shifted lines, and perfected wording. Finally, it was done. The editor flew back to New York with *Oh, the Places You'll Go* in a box on her lap.

When Random House published it in 1990, the staff held their breath. Would it sell? It was another Seuss for adults. Or it might be given to children. It would be a nice book for high school or college graduates, too. But would it be successful?

The book went right onto the *New York Times* best-seller list. It stayed there for two full years. Everyone, it seemed, wanted this last piece of Dr. Seuss wisdom.

At eighty-seven, Ted stayed home sick. He puttered around his office when he could. He signed books and wrote a few letters. There were papers to put in order. He was weak and in pain. He slept a lot. A special bed was moved into his office. He could lie back in comfort and look out over the Pacific Ocean through the huge windows.

A neighbor moved in to help Audrey with Ted's nursing care. One afternoon, Ted called Audrey to his bedside. He handed Theophrastus to her. His old toy dog's fur was worn and soft, but its eyes were still shiny. "You will take care of the dog, won't you?" he asked.

The next day, September 24, 1991, Ted died in his sleep in his office.

The news spread quickly around the world. People everywhere remembered their favorite Seuss book from their childhood. Parents wept that night as they read bedtime stories by Dr. Seuss to their children.

The United States government printed a postage stamp with Dr. Seuss's face. More movies were made of his books. The huge Dr. Seuss National Memorial Sculpture Garden was created in Springfield, Massachusetts. It has life-sized statues of the characters from Ted Geisel's books. Ted is there, too, sitting at his drawing board. He has one foot up on the table, but there is still room for you to fit on his lap.

The best Dr. Seuss monuments can be found on bookshelves worldwide. Ted wrote forty-four books. More than two hundred million copies of them have been sold. They have been printed in twenty different languages. His books, worn and tattered with use, are in every school and library. Any time children open those books, they will be lost in Ted's zany world. They will learn a little more about reading, a little more about life, and they will have to smile. That is their gift from Ted Geisel.

For More Information

TO READ

For younger children:

Krull, Kathleen.
  *The Boy on Fairfield Street: How Ted Geisel
  Grew Up to Become Dr. Seuss.*
  Random House: New York, NY, 2004.
  A great introduction.

Weidt, Maryann.
  *Oh, the Places He Went: A Story
  about Dr. Seuss.*
  Carolrhoda Books: Minneapolis, MN, 1994.
  A very readable, well-researched
  description of Geisel's life.

Wheeler, Jill C.
  Dr. Seuss.
  Abdo & Daughters: Edina, MN, 1993.

A simple picture book with clear photos of places and people important to Theodor Geisel.

For art students of any age:

Cohen, Charles D.
The Seuss, the Whole Seuss, and Nothing but the Seuss: A Visual Biography of Theodor Seuss Geisel.
Random House: New York, NY, 2004.
Written for adults, but with hundreds of Geisel's sketches and cartoons, advertisements, and illustrations from childhood on, clearly showing the genesis of his ideas.

For adults:

Morgan, Judith and Neil Morgan.
Dr. Seuss & Mr. Geisel: A Biography.
Da Capo Press: Cambridge, MA, 1996.
Thorough, respectful coverage of all the events in Geisel's life.

TO WATCH

A&E Biography *Dr. Seuss*

TO VISIT

The Dr. Seuss National Memorial
Sculpture Garden, Springfield, MA. After you
have touched all the life-sized bronze statues,
there are exhibits next door at the Connecticut
Valley Historical Museum. You can also visit
the Zoo at Forest Park where Ted's father
worked, drive down Mulberry Street, and see
buildings that inspired many of Ted's settings.

The Geisel Library at the University of California
at San Diego contains thousands of illustrations
and papers from Theodor Geisel's life.

Dartmouth College, Theodor Geisel's almmater.
Look at the buildings and visit his collections
in the library.

ONLINE

http://www.catinthehat.org/index.html is the
   Dr. Seuss National Memorial Sculpture
   Garden site.
www.seussville.com This enormous, colorful
   "Seussville" site is maintained by Random
   House, the publisher of Ted's books.

THE THEODOR GEISEL BOOKS
How many have *you* read?
Books written and illustrated by Dr. Seuss:

And to Think that I Saw It on Mulberry Street, 1937
The 500 Hats of Bartholomew Cubbins, 1938
The Seven Lady Godivas, 1939, repr 1987
The King's Stilts, 1939
Horton Hatches the Egg, 1940
McElligot's Pool, 1947
Thidwick, the Big-Hearted Moose, 1948
Bartholomew and the Oobleck, 1949
If I Ran the Zoo, 1950
Scrambled Eggs Super!, 1953

Horton Hears a Who!, 1954
On Beyond Zebra, 1955
If I Ran the Circus, 1956
The Cat in the Hat, 1957
How the Grinch Stole Christmas, 1957
The Cat in the Hat Comes Back, 1958
Yertle the Turtle and Other Stories, 1958
Happy Birthday to You!, 1959
One Fish Two Fish Red Fish Blue Fish, 1960
Green Eggs and Ham, 1960
The Sneeches and Other Stories, 1961
Dr. Seuss's Sleep Book, 1962
Dr. Seuss's ABC, 1963
Hop on Pop, 1963
Fox in Socks, 1965
I Had Trouble in Getting to Solla Sollew, 1965
The Cat in the Hat Songbook, 1967
The Foot Book, 1968
I Can Lick 30 Tigers Today! and Other Stories, 1969
I Can Draw It Myself, 1970
Mr. Brown Can Moo! Can You?, 1970
The Lorax, 1971
Marvin K. Mooney, Will You Please Go Now!, 1972
Did I Ever Tell You How Lucky You Are?, 1973
The Shape of Me and Other Stuff, 1973
There's a Wocket in My Pocket!, 1974
Oh, the Thinks You Can Think!, 1975

The Cat's Quizzer, 1976
I Can Read with My Eyes Shut, 1978
Oh Say Can You Say?, 1979
Hunches in Bunches, 1982
The Butter Battle Book, 1984
You're Only Old Once!, 1986
Oh, the Places You'll Go!, 1990

Books written by Dr. Seuss
and illustrated by others:

Gerald McBoing Boing, 1951
Great Day for Up, 1974
I Am Not Going to Get Up Today!, 1987

Books written by Theo. LeSieg:

Ten Apples Up On Top!, 1961
I Wish That I Had Duck Feet, 1965
Come Over to My House, 1966
The Eye Book, 1968
My Book About Me, 1969
I Can Write! A Book by Me, Myself, 1971
In a People House, 1972
The Many Mice of Mr. Brice, 1973
Wacky Wednesday, 1974
Would You Rather Be a Bullfrog, 1975

Hooper Humperdink . . . ? Not Him!, 1976
Please Try to Remember the First of Octember!, 1977
Maybe You Should Fly a Jet! Maybe You Should Be a Vet!, 1980
The Tooth Book, 1981

Books written as "Rosetta Stone":

Because a Little Bug Went Ka-Choo!, 1975

Books written by Dr. Seuss, then
illustrated and published after he died:

Daisy-Head Mayzie, 1994
My Many-Colored Days, 1996
Hooray for Diffendoofer Day!, 1998

184